UTOPIA

ARABIA

THE SWING SET

SERIES

BOOK THREE

KAREN MELISSA GENGE

Published by New Generation Publishing in 2017

Copyright © Karen Melissa Genge 2017

First Edition

The author asserts the moral right under the Copyright, Designs and Patents Act 1988 to be identified as the author of this work.

All Rights reserved. No part of this publication may be reproduced, stored in a retrieval system or transmitted, in any form or by any means without the prior consent of the author, nor be otherwise circulated in any form of binding or cover other than that which it is published and without a similar condition being imposed on the subsequent purchaser.

www.newgeneration-publishing.com

CHAPTER ONE

"Hi, my name is Sherie I am married to Jesus Henry William. We are floating satirically down on a cloud of euphoric love into Saudi Arabia, as a Queen and King of the Jews."

Twenty five years ago we got together on a Swing-Set playing as friends and neighbours.

Coming over from Pakistan in 2315 at 5 years old I'd been a Muslim princess with my family ready to emigrate so that my brother, Ahmed, at 17 years old could get set up through an arranged marriage to an Arabian princess. We actually moved into Palatial grounds to be integrated in to the William's family.

Now mum and dad booked my siblings into the local posh private school called Utopia.

The first day there I met Luke, Matthew, Mark and John and Ruth, Rachel and Esther. I also met my new teacher Levi of whom was a man. I clicked with this group straight away. There were only sixteen more children in class. I sat down on the many cushions near the front of the room in my very bright girly clothes. There was no one else there but a boy who came in late called Jesus. I looked straight at him and he smiled. I bowed my head along with all the other children as Levi announced that this was prince Jesus H. William and he was the one of whose family who'd brought us all together. Us girls had been called as possible suitors for all the saints and Jesus in the future. It had to be understood Levi had said that this school was for an elite group only.

My lineage was in farming, the other girls like Ruth had been in banking along with Rachel her twin sister. Esther had actually grown up as a little lady that her parents were of true blue blood from Pakistan. The other girls had to be aware from such a young age as five that this was a school set up for arranged marriages in the future. I trained myself not to look at my favourite lad straight away of whom was Jesus. I had to play the game the adults way.

Another adult came in the room and her name was Kara a chaperone for me, Esther, Rachel, Ruth, Jesus, Mark, Luke and Peter.

Then two more adults came in turn. There was one called Karen as a chaperone Levi had said was for John, Matthew, Bartholomew and Thomas with Catherine, Mary, Marie and Lucy.

The other adult was St James who was to chaperone the rest of the group for the whole year. At which point we had to stand up while a servant put our cushions round in circles in three different corners of the room. When our names were called we had to sit down in our respective groups.

Then a picture rolled down from the wall. it was an atlas and we burst in to song each introducing ourselves and where we came from as we all had to see where on the map, Levi set out in front of us where we'd all originated from. I stuck out my neck and sang proudly that I came from Pakistan. I sang the Koran prayer as well that no-one ever knew the actual words to and everyone was very impressed. Some cheeky idiot said, "There's no wailing wall in here." He was the last man to step in to the room called Mohammed. We had to stand up and bow and curtsy to our headmaster.

"Children from five different continents I welcome you as new Jewish Arabians to be princes and princesses. You will learn the Quran in the first year, then the Old Testament for two years. Then you'll be able to enjoy the New Testament full of mysteries for you to unravel as you grow up."

We had to shake hands with the founders of the school Graham Oliver Davidson and Eve Lineth-Marie Davidson and that was our first morning over with before we went outside to have a tour round the huge palace grounds on the back of a little train just for children. The last stop was a huge Swing Set Park, set up for a hundred children. There were five sets of baby swings and five sets of older children swings. Two large climbing frames, one for babies and the other for the older children. There were several slides and three roundabouts and about half a dozen see-saws. There was also an elephant, a kangaroo, a monkey, a lion, and a horse that were bouncy things on coils for the babies and toddlers. There was a huge playing field nearby and a large duck pond at the bottom. Half-way down the field was a large bandstand. Mohammed said there would be music there every evening and a big swing set band playing there every Sunday afternoon.

All us children said "Wow." Together at the park.

"Would you all like to play now?" said Graham Oliver Davidson and in unison the whole class said "Yes." We ran down from the palace to have a go and I nearly tripped over my feet.

Luckily dress code for school was casual like denim jeans and t-shirts with sneakers on. We had a lot of fun for the rest of the day. The sun shone down upon us and Eve promised us sunshine every day for the rest of our lives.

Once at the park I had a go at everything. First the swings and the slide. I chatted endlessly to Ruth and Rachel while on the roundabout while the boys tried to dominate clambering on all around us and Jesus was left to push. I jumped off like a cat on all fours, pulled myself up and pushed the roundabout with him with barely a scratch on myself. Jesus and I spoke to each other about how great the place was.

"Of course it is Sherie my parents King Joseph and Queen Mary own the place. Thanks for helping me." He laughed a big boom of a laugh at me. He looked so proud and puffed out his chest. "Aren't you looking forward to being bridesmaid at your brother Ahmeds wedding in a year's time to my sister Sara?"

"Of course, but I love living in each moment to moment and try to prevent each inevitable disaster I meet along the way. Things like wonderful weddings I will deal with, as momma says, along the way."

Looking at everyone else playing made Jesus and I happy. We even went to help push the babies in their prams around the field down to the pond afterward. Once there we found bread underneath the buggies and shared it round to throw at the ducks, that went "quack, quack" that Jesus and I with others tried to copy. As one waddled off Jesus put his finger to his lips to say, "Ssh," as he grabbed me with his other hand to go look at the remaining eggs. We stood there in awe with running children coming down from the swing sets through the trees. Some of them were chasing squirrels. I thought like "Wow," I couldn't believe the freedom being felt in the air all about me. Soon all the children were throwing bits of bread to all the winged creatures. The pond was huge with a little island in the middle.

Other families were there beside us with their friends. The park had been packed with people but time and space descended in to one special moment between Jesus and I as we picked up a poorly bird between us. Jesus laid his healing hands on the bird's legs and I shivered with excitement expecting a miracle. His hand glowed all pink and we stayed in that pose which seemed to go on forever and when he let go the lame bird hobbled a bit before flying off. From then on in, Jesus was my healing the animals, friend. I actually asked him how he did it.

"It takes great control and patience with inner prayers."

"I'd love to do that too." And out the corner of my eye Karen was watching us standing with James looking really happy together sharing what looked like a private little joke. I decided there and then to start doing the same with Jesus.

"I'm gonna call you Jesus the healer," my eyes smiled up at him and I'd never felt so alive and free from constraints knowing a little miracle was always gonna come my way, right from there on in with Jesus.

"I'll call you Sherie the healer." Jesus said to me, "If you let me teach you."

"I'd love that." I said, "I wanna be a vet in the future with healing hands like yours."

"That's what I plan on being too." He said.

About five thirty everyone started back towards the palace and we all said our goodbyes as we spread out all over the inside of the palace walls to the family areas of where we were now to call home.

Back in my quarters with my brother Ahmed and mum and dad, Ashran and Aaron, I started getting ready for tea. A maid had been in our living quarters and had made a lovely paella ready for us steaming hot on the table. The whole family loved this dish with a bit of salmon. I nibbled the food whilst cross-legged on a cushion on the floor eating with chopsticks.

"Mmm." I went. "Guess who I made friends with today mum."

"Well loads of children I'll bet!"

"Mainly Jesus." I'd said.

"I hope the appropriate chaperone was with you."

"Well a lovely lady called Kara looked over at us mamma but so did the other chaperones as we were all together today. Did you know where we originally came from? Apparently in Asia. There are children from all over the world here mum."

"Did you meet an Inuit?"

"You mean Eskimo?" I bit my bottom lip, put my finger across my mouth with my thumb underneath and said, "I think Kara my chaperone was one mum. What do you think of that?"

"It's alright sweet. Your mum and dad know all about the school you're in and their policies."

"Have I got to marry someone in this school though and are we ever going home?"

"Right. Firstly we came here for your brother's arranged marriage and yes we're hoping to fix you up with someone in an arranged marriage in the future also. We can go home on holidays anytime during school holidays. This is an educational establishment you know called Utopia and we just want the best for you."

"Well all I really did all day mum was learn where Pakistan is on the map. I made friends with a Ruth and Rachel from America and a really good friend with Jesus. Then we went to the biggest park I'd ever seen of where I thought this place is brilliant."

"I'm glad poppet and it is fantastic you're getting on with the other students, but this is now our home for a very long time."

"Well…," I screwed up my eyes and made a face, "If I've got to marry I'd like who you'd choose for me mum."

"As long as you've found true, true love that's all we care about." Said dad who'd just come in to the room after having his evening shower. "You get on well with Jesus then yeah?" he said sidling up to me on the sofa.

"Yes dad. I think him and girls named Ruth and Rachel from America really like me. Can I have an arm wrestle dad?"

"Sure you can." He held his arm up really well as I grabbed his hand but I needed both of mine to push his arm over.

"Well done love." He said, "Now scoot upstairs. Get your jammies on and clean your teeth. You'll have an earlier start tomorrow when you go on a day trip. It says on your itinerary you're going to a safari park sometime this year."

"Will I see giraffes, elephants, rhinos, apes, gorillas and anteaters and things?"

"Yes love. I know your first day was bound to be exciting…," then he yawned, "But we all want to get to bed. Now scoot. I'm in the bathroom after you."

"Yes dad." And I soon got in to bed. In the morning I peeked out my window to a huge courtyard with exotic foliage in the middle making it look like an uninhabitable type of park but with benches outside every apartment window with a path way running along round it. I went to get in to the bath drawn up for me by a servant. Dad had insisted on loads of bubbles of which I just jumped in to and swam like a little fish in this huge bath tub. I had bath scrubbies, oils, lotions, loads of soap and shampoo and conditioners all around me. This was pure heaven.

Half an hour later mum came in and told me to get out as Ahmed wanted to get in to fresh water. I dived under the water to pull the plug out. I laughed and gurgled and a lady in a starch uniform held out a bath sheet for me to step in to. Nice and cosy in a warm towel I dried myself down and picked up some Dove spray to smell ultra-nice with after that wonderful bath.

In the school room sat at a desk I had a rubber and a pencil to draw my family. I drew mum and dad and Ahmed. Then I put their names over the top of the picture. I was very pleased with myself. I signed it and dated it.

The next lesson I was on a cushion again reading about Noah's Ark. I wanted to be on that boat sailing around the world helping with the animals. "I am going to be a vet." I'd said in my head. Jesus sat next to me that morning as I read my favourite passage out loud about the dove coming back with a branch between his teeth. When I sat down I drew the Ark with the animals poking their heads out of the portholes, the water and the birds. I drew a big picture of Noah with a staff in his hand.

"Is this really in the Quran?" I asked.

The teacher Levi replied, "No talking in class please. The reason we put the curriculum in that is because their testaments are books, 1, 2, and 3. The order in which it is taught doesn't matter we'll deal with the more adult themes as you get older."

I grinned, turned my book over and it said The Koran. I got confused this was an Old Testament story it said in the contents list and realised that all three books were put together inside one cover. The book in its entirety was labelled the Holy Bible encapsulating all official religious doctrines covering the Christian faith. It was a huge book and at the back the last page was number one thousand and five hundred. I flicked back and forth looking at lovely colour pictures while dreaming of going to the park later.

The next lesson was taken up in learning how to write our names. Kara helped guide my hand with the pencil in to write S-h-e-r-i-e, M-a-r-i-e, K-u-m-a-r. I then had to copy it on ten lines underneath. My hand wobbled a bit and missed a few lines as I couldn't keep the letters straight.

I looked up satisfied afterwards putting my pencil down on the desk by my work and sat there quietly with my hands on my lap.

It was three thirty and the bell went. I had a choice to join after school club to learn ballet. I'd heard of the words double pliat and desperately wanted to know what it was so I put my hand up when they asked who was gonna stay. Seven children put their hands up. The rest were to stay for one more lesson in geography that I said I already got anyway about where I lived. The extra lesson repeated from the day before was to help others to catch up and get them to understand once more.

I had to find a spare tutu and a little wrap around cardigan that the school provided all brand new and amazingly in my size. I got led to a room with parquet flooring in, a big mirror against the back wall and two wooden bars. One along the mirror and one in the middle of the room. Us little ones had to grab the bar by the mirror to start learning stretching techniques in order to limber up before learning simple steps. I piped up. "Mrs Tothill can I learn a double pliat?"

She laughed and said, "We'll get to it today. It's two simple moves from a pliat with your feet to a double one making the second move."

I lightly blushed and tilted my head to the left and put my arm over my head extending my fingers and my other arm about a foot away from encircling my body. We were then told to try and go up on tippy-toes. I wobbled and caught the bar then tried again and got it second time. The teacher told us to hold it and she passed by all of us quickly and said good girl to each of us but guided our arms as she passed in to swan like arms.

This made me happy as Jesus had put his name down for it too and got told good boy with Matthew. In my little world everybody was equal and there was good in everyone but I started to train my mind fully on what I was doing trying to do exactly what I'd told Jesus I'd do. Live in each moment to moment.

The lesson took an hour and I smelled a bit but got changed in to my jeans and t-shirt. For company I went to Jesus and said, "Do you go through the Swing Set Park to get back to your living quarters?"

"No." he said, "But I'll gladly walk through the park with you to where you live in the outer courtyards of the grounds. Can you remember how to get there from yesterday?"

"I think so." I said, "I've got to remember 27B."

"Look." He said. H waved his arms to what looked like members of staff it was Kara and James. "Do you want them both with us?" he said.

I said, "Not really."

"They've got to keep fifty yards away from us all the time."

"Right both." I'd said "because I know Kara chaperones my new friends Ruth and Rachel. Besides I think James likes staying with Karen's group."

"Alright we'll have both." He'd said. "But their adults they'll decide."

Out towards the edge of the grounds, I spied the swings first.

"Not them." Jesus said, "Let's hit the see-saw and then do the roundabout again. I loved pushing it around with you yesterday."

While on the see-saw I spied to the left a few sand dunes with bits of grass on and a few palm trees and behind them were big white walls. I asked Jesus what was behind them.

He said, "The camel park. There's going to be a field trip there one day. I just know it and we'll traipse around the perimeters of the palace grounds, that's all sand, as we live in the middle of the Sahara."

"I'd rather show off my animal control techniques by riding them around inside the grounds." Said James of whom butted in. "I've been trying to change the rules about the day trip through bugging Graham Oliver Davidson."

"But perhaps you should try bugging my parents King Joseph and Queen Mary of the Jews instead."

"I've got to go home." I said, "Mum'll be waiting."

Jesus puffed out his chest and said, "Believe me if they thought we'd spent a lot of time together they'd be euphoric.

"Oh yes 'cause you're the best Jesus Christ above all other's right?"

"You're the first one to take the piss." He said and we jumped off the swings together as we parted company and Kara guided me back to my living quarters that I was beginning to call home.

By the Saturday I'd settled in to a new routine and I was beginning to like the cushions on the floor of which were never used that way at home. This was the first time I'd ever encountered an educational establishment in my life. Mum would still tell me off if I threw cushions on the floor. I decided to pick up my prayer mat to place in the living room facing east with my family and I made the Quran prayer come out singing loudly. I was always happiest during prayers.

Afterwards there was a knock on the door and I calmly and in control opened the door to Jesus with Kara asking for a date. I had to ask mum if I could go out. She beamed at me.

"Of course you can Sherie. Just be back by five o'clock. You can't skip too man y prayer times today, but you've got our blessing." She said to Kara and mum bowed her head in reverence to Jesus. "May I have itinerary please?" she asked.

"It will be a day in the park with a picnic." That is all Kara said.

Mum gave me a hug. Looked at me stern in the face and tilted my chin up. "You'll do." She said, "But don't go out without your veil."

I said, "Sure mum. I wouldn't dishonour the family." Then said "Thank you." And bowed my head in compliance with what was to come. We were allowed traditional prayer days and ethnic foods from home on the weekend. Mum gave us home-made samosas to take with us she'd prepared while I'd been at school.

"You shan't need much sweetheart. I love you."

"I love you too mum. Have a good day."

At the Swing Set Park, 'cause that's what it's called, we walked through by the aviary at the bottom, over a little bridge, and over to the wooden tables there with attached benches either side. It was then that Kara opened quite a large wicker hamper with plates, knives, forks, spoons, napkins and a flask in. There was lots of food too. I got offered PG Tips tea from the flask.

"Do you like milk?" Kara asked me.

I said "Yes please."

I'd dressed up that morning in a long flowing dress that was brightly coloured and beautiful. I had to lift my veil they'd said for Jesus to see my face. The face that he'd said looked beautiful when he first saw me at school.

His chaperone got out some Victoria sponge to go with our tea as Jesus said it was elevenses. I nib bled at the small slice of cake and so did Jesus. We made elevenses last as long as we could.

"How do you like my park?" he'd said.

"It's beautiful and there's certainly a lot to do here."

"I've asked if we could spend the best part of the day here. Say when you'd like to go home." That choice was very gracious and full of gratuitness. I was happy to be out with a friend. I was going to make the most of the day.

We chatted non-stop about our families. I told him all about my sisters Fee and Eve. He told me that he had two sisters. I then mentioned my brother Ahmed born traditionally in to a Muslim family, ours. I told him of how my dad had been a widower after his first wife died years ago. It was seven years later he found his second wife Ashran and they gave birth to Fee, me, then Eve.

Jesus told me all about Elizabeth and Sara his sisters and Josh and Jacob were his twin younger brothers.

We talked and talked for what seemed hours about our families until making our way to the see-saw. We exhausted poor Kara after pushing the see-saw up and down for ages and then pushing the swings for us.

Jesus and I had a light lunch at 2 o'clock. I'd had my samosa with crisps and chocolate and he had unlevened bread ready for the ducks he'd said. Kara interjected. "You're supposed to eat that for lent."

"Do you mean the Passover?"

"In a way yes." Our chaperone said. We were going to have to learn about each other's faiths or just talk about one common faith Christianity but I liked to educate this King of the Jews to be.

Jesus and I talked on about family for most of the afternoon. I looked up to Kara briefly as she looked at her watch. "It's time to go on Miss Sherie. We'll escort you back home."

I think my first date with a boy had gone brilliantly.

Now that day Matthew and Luke had dates too with two girls from St James group and I recognised them doing the same thing around us except they'd played ball games and used Frisbees and took pet dogs on their dates. I felt very grown up as I'd described my afternoon to my mother as all we'd done really was picnicked, used the swing sets and shared stories all day. Mum seemed pleased.

Now on a Sunday we had to go to a Christian catholic church to be integrated into other groups of worshippers of God. All our suitors were there along with other boys and girls from our older peers in years two and three at school.

In church there were just an empty golden cross at the front of the church and a statue of mother Mary with her baby Jesus in her arms. This part of the Christian faith seemed to emulate the Virgin Mary higher than anyone else. We always emulated Jesus as the highest of others to over inflate the ego of. I got involved in the service as I'd asked in the beginning if there was anything I could do to help. They said that I could help with the coffees after the service in the hall upstairs. I beamed inside feeling that I could be useful and being particularly able to talk about my original faith. The family one to these people.

I said, "Why are these people in the congregation over emphasising every single word of the Lord's Prayer as I don't understand the meaning of trespasses?" I asked the vicar and he told me it was just a fancy word for sin. I loved the service but had to cover my face that morning with my veil. I'd sat with my brother and two sisters and I soon took to one special hymn called Onward Christian Soldiers, a nice powerful tune with very important messages to march along to as we'd walked in to the church. In the service I'd enjoyed the sermon with a powerful message about turning the other cheek whilst they emulated all those who fought for peace.

After church the children all went to the Swing Set Park in the glorious sunshine. The grass was a bit wet. They said it had rained in the middle of the night. I saw several prickly plants and my mother said they were called cacti. I had a go on the swings and I liked to twist the chains around as tight as they would go before letting go and spinning around ever so fast making me feel really giddy but giving me a lovely thrill. I done this over and over again until I'd had enough. Then I went to the very high slide. I climbed to the top and felt a little bit wobbly before sitting down in my jeans and sneakers with a bright red sari on top of my t-shirt. I wanted to look like a modern Muslim girl. I soon shot down to the bottom and my mum and dad went weee..., just for me. I was a bit mortified as the other children turned round and stared at me. I felt embarrassed but gutted it out and then went to the roundabout to push my friends round and round on it. Jesus and I jumped on the see-saw together afterward and we laughed as our parents stood and watched at least the chaperones weren't needed today. I had to tell him that I was going on a date that Friday afternoon with a boy named Peter.

CHAPTER TWO

It was Friday morning I'd been living in Arabia for nearly two whole weeks and was starting to feel a little bit home sick. I had to put up with a Chinese young lad saying I was a horse.

I asked him, "What are you on about?"

He said that he studied calendars and that the year I was born it had been the year of the horse. I thought that that had been a bit strange, but I knew that to be respectful I had to accept our differences. I wandered what the horses attributes actually were. It gave me an idea during free play to ask if we could make horses together. My idea was to use old broom sticks. Take the ends off, stuff socks and tie them on to the old brooms. Then stick a mouth, eyes and ears on to be able to have races with up at the park later. The teacher thought it was a good idea to do as an extra-curricular class after school on the Monday and said they'd have to buy the brooms first for all the children in my class. I farted and felt mortified gladly no-one realised and they all just glazed over it and thankfully ignored me so as not to cause more embarrassment for me. It had been right in the middle of a lesson and I prayed that Peter never heard and that I didn't smell. This afternoon's date had actually been asked for by me two days after my date with Jesus went well. I needed to get to know the boys in my year I told the teachers. Levi was impressed and asked me why Peter? I replied that I fancied him but was going to be a bit shy around him unless I had some me-time with Peter.

"How would you like to crack the ice?" Levi asked.

"Well when I went out with Jesus he'd mentioned there being a camel park just outside the grounds."

"It's a good idea." Levi said "But I've noticed you and Peter. You barely talk beyond polite niceties."

"That's because he makes me feel tongue-tied and very aware of myself. I feel like I'd like to know him better if we're all supposed to grow up together to be each other's suitors."

The teacher said she was always impressed with my behaviour as well as my work. Now I knew that Peter came from England and that his ancestors had set up a large fishing company that hauled millions of fish to send to shops and supermarkets all over the world, but I needed to know him personally. I squirmed in my seat. I had an hour to whip home and put on my best clothes and my veil. Mum said the veils weren't necessary anymore but I didn't want to show off my constantly blushing face. That was fine my mother had said but at a camel park I'd have to dress more appropriately so I had to put trousers on a silk chemise. I felt all grown-up. I grabbed a brush to put my long hair up in to a pony tail just as the door rang and Peter turned up with his chaperone in tow, Kara.

"Hi, I know you know my heritage and I know yours as your lineage is the farmers range of wholesale foods, but I'd love to know you personally too. I've actually been pestering Kara to set up a date with you."

I bowed my respectful little head with my veil drooped around my neck I refused, to mum to give up my Muslim faith as I loved it.

Once outside I could sense a sandstorm coming. Kara then pre-emptied my question. "It's ok, I've managed to re-arrange the route the camels take to carry you two around the King and Queen of the Jews grounds."

"That's great." I'd said, "I've heard that you're a fixer-upper. I thought it was just to do with date fixing."

"Right." Kara said, "I'm glad you've stuck with Muslim tradition though as the camel park is still outside the grounds in the middle of a sand storm. The veil will protect your poor throat from lots of sand down it. You need sunglasses as well though."

Now Peter knew about my faith and was a Christian but got prepared by humouring who I was and what I was about by getting his own veil to cover his mouth with.

"Don't worry." He'd said. "I find myself blushing around you too."

"But," I'd said, "Boys and men don't wear veils."

"Integration is the word here, mind." Said Kara, butting in. As a laugh we covered our faces anyway before getting on elephants with cushy seats on top to take us to the camel park.

Kara butted in, "I hope you've got a picnic tea this time."

"Don't worry," I'd said. "I've anticipated this date for two whole weeks and spent time over the contents of our picnic."

"Is that why we were told not to bring one?" said Peter.

"Yes." I'd said, "We have a lovely mixture of Indian foods including my favourite vegetarian samosas and don't worry Peter we looked up about sushi just in case you liked it."

"I love sushi." He said, "Uncooked fish sounds lovely."

We soon jumped on the elephants that were outside in the courtyards tethered up and ready to walk us through the Swing Set Park. Sat up high it felt wonderful parading by all the boys and girls happily filling the whole park. I farted again getting redder by the minute at least everyone could assume the smell came from the elephants. One pooed by the bandstand and there was a servant ready to pick it up with a poop-scoop and threw it on to the mud around the stand to help fertilise the bushes and flowers surrounding it. The swing set band were there and they started playing Nellie the Elephant.

"Packed her trunk and trundled off to the circus." I sang to myself. Peter looked across from the other elephant and laughed. Then said, "Oh I know that one." And the song radiating around the park officially broke the ice for us. We just giggled and sang the rest of the nursery song between us.

At the camel park we were ordered to put on the veils anyway as we clambered on Branston and Bryce the camels. Mine was called Bryce.

"Giddy up Bryce." I'd said trying to dig my heels in to the side of him.

"Don't bother." Said the trainer, "We'll lead the way."

I desperately wanted to talk to Peter at that point proudly talking about Andromidi but we couldn't shout to each other so we both got walked around the perimeters of the palace grounds. It took three hours to go round the beaten track before we all converged back in the park again after we'd alighted back where we started. I'd prayed to Allah on the camel dead scared at first but I felt strangely elated when we got off.

A picnic blanket came out of my trunk, no pun intended, that had been laid on the grass by Kara of whom had stayed behind. The little knives and forks and plates were laid out ready for tea. The food was delicious and Peter and I sang old nursery rhymes together intermittently in between talking about our families. I was really getting to know him. I'd fancied him for ages and boasted of my cooking skills.

"I've got some unlevened bread to share with you." He said. "We've all got to get used to it for fasting for forty days and forty nights just before Easter."

"Oh I know that one." I'd said. "Jesus explained all about it two weeks ago I have to eat kosher meats." I'd said, "But I'm a vegetarian anyway."

We broke the bread anyway and it tasted delicious. At seven o'clock Kara tapped her watch and I bowed as I stood up. "Thank you so much for this afternoon Peter. I'd really looked forward to this and it didn't disappoint." I took Kara's hand and walked off to my living quarters, that was beginning to feel more and more like home.

Now Mohammed came to see me that evening at eight o'clock and he insisted on chatting to mum and dad with me and my brother. He needed to find out if we practiced the prayers to Mecca. I'd said, "Yes. I love my Muslim traditions."

"I hope you can understand, 'cause I pray to God more these days than to Allah for it is a cardinal sin to pray to that man."

"Why what bad things could actually happen to me?"

"Physically nothing but all Muslims will have to pray to God one day as it says in the Ten Commandments to love God your only God for he goes by no other name."

I didn't want to apologise for my prayers, "But," I said. "I do practice the Lord's Prayer that was introduced to me in the Catholic Church service last Sunday."

"I am the Mohammed founder of the Muslim faith and I beg you stick to praying to God, and Jesus please or I've done something seriously wrong. You can pray to Saint James if you want. But don't emulate that man's name ever again."

"I don't want to shame my family. I'll try harder. I promise." And a little tear fell out of my right eye over my cheek. "You told us we were chosen for a reason in my mother's letters and I quote it's not just because of Ahmed's up and coming wedding is it? I'm a good girl my parents have always told me."

"I'm only asking you to change one thing or you'll get shipped back home on your own we don't need certain prayers said."

I wanted to throw the mother of all tantrums ever and I found myself stamping my foot hard on the ground. "That's not fair." I screamed expecting mum to back me up but it looked like they were all against me. "It's my faith and you're not screwing with it. I deserve the chance to be here and marry someday a wonderful Prince of the Jews." I exhaled hard and counted to ten in the back of my mind and walked out in a strop.

"I wanted to stop this tirade of abuse. I am the Mohammed and I only ever prayed to God. I assure you. One thing only you're getting wrong. You are a good girl and we're trying to keep the best of each religion at this school."

I bowed low and said, "I'm sorry sir." My mother then stepped in. "Look my daughter had never had a tantrum before and I will reprimand her my way. Believe me sir it will not happen again. I will personally see to it."

I burst in to tears and said. "I'm sorry." Yet again, "It won't happen again."

"Consider this a warning then and your singing prayers to Mecca are lovely but train your mind to think of God and you'll emulate yourself even higher."

"Thank you."

"You can call me Mohammed you know if you like ma'am or should I say Mrs Kumar?"

"Mrs Kumar please. I wish we could have met over better circumstances. We are very well welcomed here all the time."

I then gave mum a cuddle after my headmaster left. "I'll still call him sir though mum. I promise."

"Silly girl. He meant your father and I could say it."

I smiled up at her. "Go and get ready for bed we are having such a lovely time always remember so keep being gracious. Let that side of you shine dear."

A few months later I'd pretty much made dates several times with the boys in my year at school. Life was rosy. The Palace grounds were the size of the whole of England to me as I'd learned that every modern pass time seemed to exist here and I loved every minute.

At six years old I could competently ride a horse all of my own and was out cantering about with my favourite Cobbles. On the other horses were Jesus and Kara. I'd managed to talk them in to riding around the inside perimeter of the Swing Set grounds. Reigning in on Cobbles straining at the bit to gallop I managed to stay close to Jesus and our chaperone Kara. I'd lost count at how many times Jesus had asked me on dates and how many times I'd asked the other boys out. All I'd ever thought of was keeping my options open just like my parents had told me to. I still prayed five times a day on Saturdays and wore my veil in free time. I'd even acquired my own hair stylist as my mum knew all the staff around the palace by now by name. She made me keep firstly a diary and a notebook to a) put birthdays in of my class and anniversaries of the adults that were chaperoning as well as mum and dads. The notebook I kept was a daily record of achievement.

I thought about this as I hacked around the perimeters of the Swing Set Park. I happily rode with my nose stuck in the air as I'd just made it as an equestrian dressage. Jesus and I were practicing for the under elevens year old annual Olympics. It had been getting harder to make dates with lads as Jesus wanted my company more and more. I really loved talking to him too the more time I spent in his company.

We alighted our horses and tethered them up back at the equestrian centre. "Do you want to go to lunch?" I asked.

Jesus replied, "I'd love to. Where would you like to go?"

"Down at the Oasis the local shopping precinct to dine at Burger King."

"That's fine. My mother will be there meeting with my brothers and sisters this afternoon. Would you like to be introduced?"

I leapt at the chance and begged Kara to go with us. She said "No. After I take you there you'll be left with an appropriate adult anyway to bring you home."

I said "Thank you Kara. You're a good friend." Jesus and I patted the horses and one seemed to be a bit lame. Jesus healed the animal's leg with the power of prayer while I'd been left to put a warm hand over the area for ten minutes. By this time we'd become a healing team. We knew that we could make animals well but the stable manager still insisted on bringing out the vet, so we left them to it as Jesus and I jumped in to the nearest jeep to head off for the local Oasis shopping precinct about two miles away.

When we pulled up I got a surprise Mr and Mrs King of the Jews came out to greet us. This was when the jeep turned round and left us to take Kara home not that far away from there.

"Hello ma'am." I'd said but she said, "Call me Mary and call him Joseph, please."

I smiled at them and said hello to Sara, her twin sister and two other lads all of Jesus's siblings. I made a point of getting to know Sara and asked her outright.

"Is it ok if I can be your bridesmaid in a year's time?"

"I thought you'd never ask."

"Have you got a colour scheme for the wedding?"

"Funny you should say that as I've been putting together a scrapbook full of the things I want to book up for the wedding with a list of prices and things. Most things for two months' time are already booked up but I need your opinion on your bridesmaid dress. What colour is your favourite?" and she held out three swabs of shades of blue for me to choose from.

"I love the royal blue in the middle. It reminds me of a favourite top I've got."

"I'm glad you said that." She said "'Cause you'll match the others."

Two days later while walking through the Swing Sets I stopped and talked to Sara and mentioned that I liked her company and would she play on the swings with me. She said that was fine. We started kicking out in tandem as the both of us rose higher then competed with ourselves to go higher still, but seventeen year old Sara went higher than me. I dared myself to jump off really high up so I did and ended up rolling in the grass and I hurt my shoulder.

"Ow!" I screamed and everyone came rushing over. My mum had a right go at me. "You stupid girl what the hell do you think you're doing?"

Through my sobs I yelled, "But Jesus and I did this perfectly together a few months ago."

"You were barely a metre off the ground then Sherie. I don't think you realise just how high you were."

"We're going to have to take her to hospital aren't we dad?" Jesus said.

"We'll have to. Jesus can you collect any homework you can get for Sherie today please?"

"Of course I will." He sobbed. I was still shrieking out in pain. Not being able to move the ambulance came to me and I had to be lifted on to a stretcher after being given very strong painkillers. The ambulance whirred down the road near to St Saviours' hospital and pulled up to A and E.

Painfully unaware of where I was they tried to walk me in to the accident and emergency part of the hospital. They checked me over and thankfully nothing was broken but a bone had slipped out of place.

"Now what we'll do next will be even more painful." And they pushed the bone back in to place. I desperately screamed out before I passed out.

It was the next day when I saw Jesus come to see if I was ok and he asked me what was wrong. I told him that a bone in my shoulder had dislodged but got pushed back in. My arm was in a sling. he offered to heal the pain in my shoulder the same way we'd healed many animals together.

I said, "You could try." So we prayed together and I felt the heat of his hands on my left shoulder. He stayed with me all afternoon and members of my family came and went that day.

I was soon out of hospital a few days later but I was still in a sling and had been told to take things easy. I missed a trip with school to the safari park but Jesus and Kara came in with photos and cheered me up at home.

Luckily I was fine in time for my brother's wedding to Sara and we'd merged a Muslim wedding with lots of colours and a dance routine together of which I managed to take part in. The celebrations went on for two days. It was brilliant.

Three years later at nine years old I decided to be a star sign predictor and felt like a prophet as I predicted, in a dream, that a Bible that was on my night stand would lie around forever in a library called Red socks, Pink knickers, the Third Testament. I found it in somewhere called the Amethyst room. She'd said, "Yes. It's miles away from here near Texas. A young woman called Karen Genge foresaw a holistic centre to help those with emotional, spiritual and physical pains. It's written in a book called the Third Testament."

"Do you mean Red socks, Pink knickers, Third testament?"

"Well yes." She said. "How did you know?"

"I think fate has bought me here to get me a copy of that book."

"That's easy the original is at the hospital. We're going on a field trip there soon. I believe the woman maybe a distant ancestor of yours."

"How do you work that one out?" I said.

"Because there are photos of her there as the founder of the hospital and a list of her family tree in a museum near there. You might just get to add your name to it."

The rest of the class perked up. "Might we be related?"

"No." Sarai said. "You might be the soul descendant. The only one that's left."

"Why would I think that I have to study the star signs for predictions?"

"Well there are hundreds of Third Testament books that were written by sinners that turned in to saints and I believe you can trace your female line back to Katherine the Great then marrying in to the Genghis Khan line during the 20th century. Them being a part of a Simpson-Holly line of where one of your ancestors married a Fouracres and that's where it changes line again to Fouracres for two centuries before meeting up with a very old Muslim line the Kumars. In fact." Said Miss Sarai. "I want the whole class to research their ancestry trees. You can research the male lines and I'm giving you two months before the Christmas break to compile books.

The next lesson was with Saint James and we learned mathematics. We got our text books out and we had to learn about the twelve times table. At first we took turns to shout out the answers but had to say how our minds came out with them. St James said "Five times twelve is…,"

My hand soon shot in to the air. "Yes Miss Kumar."

"Well five times two is ten. Five times one is one. Add the one to the five and you get sixty."

"Thank you." He said, "For telling us your working out. Can somebody tell us another way to work it out?"

Matthew put his hand up. "I can do this on my fingers sir."

"Go on then."

"Right. One finger is twelve, two is twenty four, three is thirty six. Four is forty eight and five is sixty." He'd said as each finger went in to the air.

"How about," he'd said, "Someone come out and do their working out on the board." Ruth stuck her hand up.

"Right here's the marker. Show us how to do the sum."

"Ok sir," and she got up and put the twelve at the top then the times sign under the one and a five under the two. Then it was easy to show what I'd been on about. Mr Lloyd actually looked pleased for once and said "I'm really glad I've had three different versions of doing this sum. it shows me how you think."

By the end of the lesson he got us to do it on an abacus as well which was a wooden frame with different coloured beads on. I actually loved this lesson.

During lunch I hung out with my sisters Fee and Eve just talking over our lunch boxes. Mine had my favourite samosas in it with a packet of crisps, apple and a box drink. We sat on the steps outside the assembly hall looking down over the amazing view we had of the Swing Set Park.

After lunch my friends and I went to physical education. We wore soft and flirty little skirts and white little t-shirts with trainers on. We went outside to play baseball on an all-weather pitch. I got to choose one team and Jesus got to choose the other one. I automatically went for Ruth, Rachel, Esther, Bartholomew, Thomas, Andrew, Matthew, Simon, Leviticus, Catherine and Peter.

Jesus chose John, Mary, Luke, Marie, Lucy, Esther, Mark, Stephen, Elisabeth, Corinne, and Jamie.

After the flip of a coin I declared heads to bat first. I let out a shriek of joy when they shouted. "Yes. It's heads."

So the other team spread out across the all-weather pitch and we lined up to take the bat. We all had peaked caps to shield ourselves from the sun. I was told to take it easy and not to over extend myself as my old injury would play me up from time to time. I'd even started to learn being ambidextrous. It was only in extreme circumstances my old shoulder injury would play up anyway. The pitcher threw the ball at me and I struck out. They threw again and I recoiled from the ball fearing it would hit me. I had a third ball and my bat actually connected with it but I got caught out.

All together my team scored fifteen runs before we were all out. Then it was our turn to field and I let ball after ball fall through my fingertips as watching Peter and Jesus run around in their little shorts was putting me off.

I stood there happily really enjoying the lesson with my little face aglow knowing I'd finally got in to catching the ball which kept coming in my direction. It was like everyone kept daring me to drop it. In the end though I caught out three people and the other team got twenty runs. They won. After sweating our pants off, we all headed towards the separate boys and girls showers. I had a long hot soapy shower and got out feeling refreshed.

After physical education the school day was over and the whole school wanted to break free from all restraints of the classroom and couldn't wait to fill the Swing Set Park. I grabbed Peter's hand and we ran towards the slides and we chose the tallest one. We hogged that slide together and stopped anyone going up and down as Peter and I just sat at the top together for ages talking. It was nice and together we arranged a date for that Saturday. Peter was a normal Christian to me. He always went to the local Anglican church every Sunday and my family had found a decent Mosque to pray in every Saturday. I didn't always participate but the parishioners knew that I was graciating myself in to other faiths. As long as I could keep singing my favourite Meccan prayer and puta veil on my face once in a while as I was still proud of my Muslim faith. I was happy.

That Saturday Peter came to my abode and bought some flowers. He wafted them under my nose. It twitched and I sneezed, "Excuse me." I said. I looked into his big brown eyes, "But they're beautiful." There were six red roses and I took them straight away to find a vase. "Come on in." I told him. "Make yourself comfortable and sit on the sofa."

"I could give you a hand." He'd said. Peter looked a bit uncomfortable.

"Umm, sure." I said. "The kitchen scissors are in the drawer by the sink."

I'd then found out a nice glass vase to put them in.

"What are the scissors for?"

"Just nip off a couple of inches from the stems so that I can arrange them without the flowers sticking out too tall." I filled the vase up with water and shook the plant food packet over the water of which I gave a stir.

"That was quick Peter. Let me take over and arrange them." Of which I did and I think I started to fall in love with Peter as I just gazed at my beautiful red flowers. I looked at Peter and felt my eyes twinkling back up to him. I felt like I was drowning in his big brown eyes and felt very drawn to him. I'd always liked Peter and finally I'd asked for another date. I realised that with him I felt very romantic and mum said, "You see things through rose-tinted glass with that one."

"I know mum but I love him," mum gave me a kiss.

"You'll grow out of these crushes." She lowered her voice in my ear. "Jesus had called you again today by the way. He wants another date and so does Jamie. You'll have to choose once and for all when you're old enough."

Under my breath I'd said. "I secretly like Luke too." Mum smiled. "Your sisters get chatted up by Luke too you know."

"Yeah," I'd said, "I want to know what the fuss is all about 'cause my sisters get into scraps about him."

Dad smiled, "He's got raw sexual magnetism." And he laughed his head off. "They got more money in that family than us. They're all insurance brokers owning a global firm."

"Sure dad. Can I concentrate on this date please?"

"I like Peter." Dad said. "He's nice and down to earth but might end up a bit smelly all the time when he's older."

"You're winding me up aren't you dad?"

"Yes." He said. "It's your choice just make the most of today while he still smells nice."

"Excuse me sir." Peter said. "Do you mind I don't like being spoke about behind my back and we own the fishing trawler firm you know. I don't appreciate this. I really like your daughter and I'll ask for the next date with her after this one."

We headed out the door and Peter knew I'd missed out on the safari trip and said. "We'll take you there."

"Where?" I'd said.

"It's a surprise and all I can tell you is that you've wanted to go there for years." My mind boggled. I stupidly thought that my personal chaperone wanted a bit of a break from going out with us so I cried out loud. "I don't like surprises as long as they are nice."

"Oh, you'll love this one." Kara said. We all jumped in to the back of a jeep with a huge picnic hamper that I helped complete. I'd felt really happy and as we jostled along Peter and I started singing along together with a tape of modern songs on. We laughed about the 'Nellie the Elephant' song as well as soon as we got to outside our Utopia grounds out in to the Sahara desert. I felt a bit scared and both my feet tingled. I told Peter and he said, "That's ok. It's just a sign that you're on unfamiliar turf. I mean not literally but that you're going to experience something brand new."

I beamed up at him as he was a little bit taller than me. I didn't want to let on that I knew where we were going. Something in his expression changed, "You know where we are going don't you?"

"Hopefully the safari park." Luckily we had veils over our faces as a lot of sand was being kicked up by a breeze. I gulped and held his hands. "Can we pray together?" and for the first time in my life I prayed spontaneously the Lord's Prayer.

CHAPTER THREE

It was the safari park with lots of wide spaces enclosed by very high imposing walls to stop the sand storms coming over they'd said. As far as the eye could see there were lots of grassy areas.

"It feels unreal." I'd said. "Peter will you pinch me?" so he did on my shoulder and he said, "Pinch, punch the first of the month."

"What are you on about?" I'd said.

"It's an old saying from England as it's the first day of October. I've got in first.

Jumping down from the jeep we walked in to a booth inside a massive tourist shop and Peter paid thirty dinar for each of us to go in and I thought wow what a gentleman. He even opened the door for me at the back of the shop to lead us in to the big safari park.

Now there was a cardboard cut-out of an ape and a gorilla together with holes in where their faces should have been. I'd brought a camera and asked Kara to take a photo of both of us behind the monkeys so that our faces would have their bodies, so Peter and I could go behind the cardboard cut-outs. We grinned inanely as our photograph was taken. I was dying for a lollipop in the blistering heat. I'd covered up head to foot in long flowing garments and Peter was all dressed in white he'd said to keep him cool. I preferred dark colours and was intensely aware of the blistering heat.

"Right." I thought and looked at my map. "I take it we're near the monkey enclosure." And we strolled around straining to look up in to trees. A family in front of us were too close to a gorilla I thought as I got scared again. The guide said, "There's nothing to be afraid of." And he gave me a banana to hold out to the big ape. "Go on."

He'd said. "There's nothing to be afraid of." I quickly dangled it in front of him and Kara took a close up picture of the terror in my eyes and the banana with the ugly gorillas face nearby. I dropped the fruit last minute and ran away. Everyone laughed at me. I didn't care I had been scared to death.

The next enclosure we didn't go in and it was a family of giraffes. The guide told us that apparently they get vicious if they feel that their children are under attack.

"As if I'd attack a giraffe," I said too loudly. Peter laughed at me and I felt embarrassed glad I hadn't done this with the rest of my class. They'd have ribbed me to death forever.

"Are they deliberately keeping us out this time because giraffes smell fear?"

"No." the guide said. "It's because they'd feel under attack because they are looking after their babies. Now here's a banana. All you have to do is hold it up in to the air and the mummy will eat it straight from your hands."

I strained to look up at their faces and held my hand aloft in the air while I closed my eyes. Kara said. "Well done." Two minutes later I opened my eyes again.

"Have you got a good picture?" I'd asked.

She said, "Yes. But you have to learn Sherie how to relax."

We then went by a river and were told to just stand by the water's edge and wait. Peter held my hand. "This is so worth it just to see your face." Half an hour later I was getting bored then all of a sudden a loud noise came out from the water from a huge ugly face. It was a hippopotamus came to say hello.

"I…I don't have to feed it do I?" I stupidly asked.

"No. It's ok." The guide tried to reassure me. "Now we have to trek half a mile up the river to a bridge to take us to the lions, tigers and elephants.

"Do you feel up to it?" they said. That was Kara and the guide talking together. My eyes popped out of my head. Everyone was laughing at me.

"This isn't fair." I thought.

Peter said, "Count to ten, please. They are in enclosures. There will be a fence around them."

I then visibly sighed with a great relief. When they'd mentioned a safari in school the first time I'd thought we'd be in hot air balloons or seeing it all safely from a coach window. It was nothing of the sort and a hell of a lot of walking was involved.

Over the bridge I held on to Peter's hand and he gave my hand a reassuring little squeeze. We saw the tigers first and I decided to be a bit more daring and hung myself over the enclosure gate to try and pet one.

"They're all just members of the pussy cat family you know." I pointed out.

"You're not allowed to touch." Kara said. But I was feeling braver and then something must have spooked the tiger has he suddenly ran in my direction. I held my chest tight. it was scaring me but it suddenly stopped about ten yards away to nibble a new fresh meat lunch and all I remember is seeing blood everywhere.

Kara said to us, "Do you want to pose in front of this?"

Peter said, "Hell yes." And he took my hand and turned around with me to face the camera. I started to fidget scratching my nose through my hijab. I wanted to take it off as I actually wanted my face in the photos so I did and wrapped it around my waist. I inwardly prayed that the tiger wouldn't skulk up behind us but the photos were soon taken.

After the tigers we went to see the lions by what they called the communal water enclosure and not only did we see them but we saw some eyes come out of the water. They were alligators. I could see their bodies in the clear water and they gave me the creeps. I was sure that I was going to have a nightmare that night. We were told by the trainer to wait there while someone enticed an elephant to the water with the hope of something to eat. My heart couldn't stop racing and it took half an hour for two elephants to appear.

In front of this picture I stood looking happy for the camera again and Kara told me afterward that the alligator and the elephant came out brilliantly with me. She showed me the picture and I though "Wow!"

"We're going back to the tourist shop now and on to a nice picnic area." The guide said. I thought of Jesus birthday coming up and decided to buy him a lion peaked cap. I had plenty of money and got him a lion card too.

Jumping back in to the jeep it took us two hours to get back to the Swing Set Park to lay out in the sunshine on the grass to have our late picnic lunch. As by the time we got back it was three o'clock.

I soon tucked in to my favourite vegetarian samosas and a packet of crisps with a banana and a little boxed Robinson's drink.

Peter did the same and liked my curry flavoured samosas too.

Back at home later I felt exhausted and my mother wanted a blow by blow account of what had happened on our date. I told her about being scared of the animals and how Peter had been a perfect gentleman and helped me to confront my fears.

"I like him," Mum said "But you have a caller at five o'clock. Jesus wants to take you out for the evening."

"Oh," I'd said. "I just hope it's not a film like Madagascar or I'd be having nightmares all night. Plus I am in desperate need of a shower."

I soon jumped in to our large powered shower to take off the sand that had gone everywhere. I even washed my hair and when I'd eventually got out half an hour later and towelled my hair and put my favourite powdered blue dress on. I secretly prayed for this next date to go better than the last one. Then I soon went downstairs and had thirty minutes to spare. I picked up a Bible to study Genesis and I'd gotten to the story of Sarah and Jacob leading their family to the Promised Land. I thought why? Anywhere could have been that land and by the time they'd finished wandering for centuries they could end up back where they started anyway. They wouldn't have known they'd gone full circle several centuries on. Then there was a knock on the door. It was Jesus and I had to yell out.

"I'm just putting my sandals on and I'll be right with you."

"It's alright I'll wait in the hallway."

I came in to the hallway and asked where we were going as I rummaged through my shoes underneath the stairs. Jesus laughed, "I've got all evening you know." And my uptightness settled a little bit in to softness as I inwardly smiled. He still got my equilibrium going though I rarely ever asked for dates with him as I never really had to. He was beginning to grow on me but I wandered what Peter was doing this evening. I rarely ever stopped thinking about my Peter his voice resounded around my head in all innocence with just my own voice. I could just imagine him, as I picked up my clutch bag, saying wonderful things about how I looked if he saw me right now. I know I'd have to test him about the theatre as he said once, "'Cause I love men in tights."

Now Jesus was on time, "Punctual as usual." I'd said and grinned. "You know it's my birthday in a few days' time."

"Mine's first remember."

"Yes of course. Then we'll both be ten years old."

"It's a big deal to us and I can't wait."

"Neither can I. Mum's letting me organise my own party this year and I want a clown. Loads of friends, banners and balloons. We could do an evening shop." I said.

"Do we have to 'cause I've got plans this evening that have everything to do with my sisters' wedding. You look stunning by the way." and I blushed.

"I secretly fancy you the most." I blurted out. "But I can't stop thinking about Peter."

"Yeah well, put those thoughts on hold. We're going in my private helicopter to Tunisia for two whole days and

I have to take a servant as well as Kara and you won't be able to keep me out of your head for a change."

We walked in the palace grounds and started to explore some undergrowth until we came across a huge concreted area with the letter H on the floor underneath a big black tinted windows helicopter I got a bit scared and clambered in.

"Do you think my sisters and brother could go for a ride on this thing sometime?"

"Right. First off. this is not a thing and a pilot whose name is George is flying us to a place called Tunisia for two whole days."

"Now I forgot you have two sisters. I thought the other one was a lesbian and was going out with my older friend Faith." We laughed. "Don't worry lesbians are allowed to get married as long as they don't treat marriage like a joke."

"Of course." I'd said. "And that they make pledges to each other in a church. 'Cause in the Lord's eyes they are still Christians no matter what."

"I knew you'd say something like that." Said Jesus, "We're all children of God as long as they're willing to accept all of us with humility and respect. Do you know why I love having your company so much?"

"Not really," I'd said.

"Because you're willing to talk about anything with me."

The ride felt like a long one after that as I stared out over the Arabian princes kingdom.

"Where is Tunisia? Can I see it yet?"

"Not quite yet, but I'll tell you when you're there so that you will not get too shocked that I'm actually dodging the press for three whole days."

"Why the press?"

"Because no-one is allowed to know about this place where we are going to. It's called the Amethyst room which is a holistic centre."

"And holistic means mind, body and spiritual well-being." I had to jump in and say it myself.

"It's ok," he said, "I'd love you to have the grand tour. It's actually in the Holy City."

"I haven't read about that yet."

"I want to have a veterinary practice there soon so that we can train to be the veterinary nurses that we always wanted to be."

I leaned in for a snuggle thinking I love this friend of mine, I thought, "He remembered." And sighed. "I love this ride but it's a bit noisy!" I yelled.

He said, "I know. We're nearly there." And I looked out the window again and saw lots of buildings and on top of a sky scraper that was called the Hilton I spied a round circle and a letter H. Jesus turned to me and said "Put the headphones back on. It'll help your ears."

Kara had been quiet the whole time looking a bit pasty-faced as the helicopter roared loudly in to land. The engine soon cut off and I walked down some steps to the ground and all the time Jesus held my hand.

"I'll never forget this ever!" I shouted and Jesus smiled to me. "We're going on a private plane to a place called Arizona in America."

"Oh I know that one. Wendy in class said that she was born there."

We walked down from the roof into an elevator to take us to the ground floor of where a limousine picked us up.

"Where are we going?" I knew it was a dumb question, "Ah it's to the nearest airport, isn't it? How dumb am I." And I laughed to myself. This whole trip was amazing and about a mile outside the hub bub of the city we came across terminal six right at the edge of the Tunisian airfield. We had twenty four hours to kill before our next flight on a private plane with a man named George taking over piloting just for our privacy.

Now in Tunisia we had noodles with spiciness called jalapenos that I really loved and told Jesus so.

"How many bodyguards do you need Jesus? 'Cause I keep seeing them everywhere."

"Just the one Shaz." He said.

"Now why do you think you're starting to get hounded by the press?"

"'Cause a member of staff they're seeking out as leaked to the press all about Utopia school."

"Sounds exciting." I'd said and my heart was all of a flutter as I scoured the room behind furtive eyes.

"No-one knows me in Tunisia or cares about Christianity. I do and I don't care about groups called the anti-Christ's."

"We are never going to Sicily sometime are we? 'Cause I couldn't put up with the mafia."

I really missed Peter at this point just thinking of having a pretty normal married life. One where I'm not constantly looking over my shoulder.

Jesus pulled out a wad of notes and I shockingly recognised the face on the lowest denomination of notes and I blushed like mad and couldn't believe my date's face was on the note. The date on it was 2325.

"You're on yens! Oh my god! I can't believe who I'm dating here." I laughed, "If I marry you later on can I get my face on a note?"

"Yeah sure," he'd said with his eyebrows raising a habit he must have picked up from his dad King Joseph. I'd seen his dad do this before. I blushed again and peed my pants just a little dying of laughter in my seat.

I sipped my pink milkshake and he sipped his banana milkshake. We just both grinned at one another in the middle of McDonalds as we felt the stares of passers-by and I felt so exposed. We fell silent for a while and went to the local Hilton for a good night.

In the morning we arose from room service having slept in the penthouse suite. I'd been on a sofa bed all night. Jesus had a single bed. Kara had the king size bed to herself all night. We felt like a little family.

That afternoon we were queueing to get on a private jet to this time the destination of Arizona. In that 24 hours respite I'd called my mum and spoke to my sisters. I'd also spoken to Ahmed who lived in America. I asked Jesus on the flight.

"Are we going near San Francisco? I want to see my brother."

"Yeah I want to see my sister Sara too, but first stop is the Holy City. Now what do you know about the place?"

"Well. I'll tell you a secret. I jump several pages pass the boring parts we learn about in Revelations sometimes and I always believe that the Holy City was a real vision. But why does it say there are no buildings there when there's supposed to be one there made of jewels?"

"Right. What do you think and feel about that?"

"Well I thought that that was a bit impractical because if I walk the golden roads in wrong shoes I'll slip over and hurt my bottom or I'll scrape my arm against jewel encrusted walls." Jesus burst out laughing.

"You wouldn't want to walk on a movie set just like that vision then?" My little eyes lit up and said "Is that what we're going to see?"

"Yep, and the real Holy City."

"Please tell me it's not like the movie one?"

"No it's not." Jesus said "And only the elite few can access the place because it's all about faith in how you get there." I could feel my eyes smiling up at him as I lazed on the jet's bed and he was leaning over me. "I feel really privileged."

"You realise that you're the first girl at school that I've done this with 'cause I really trust you not so say anything about how to get to the real Holy City. But I have a duty to protect all those who travel to find it."

"Oh you mean like people travel to Lourdes?" He laughed again. "Are you laughing at me?"

"Just a little bit, but your naivety is actually going to save you from the press when we get back."

"Now tomorrow is my tenth birthday and I planned something very special to do with my girlfriend Sherie Marie Kumar."

The next day we were still on the plane and I woke up to glorious sunshine through the window that I had to push the shutter up on. The sun was so bright over many fluffy white clouds. But I just stared at it making me yawn and put the shutter down again. The comfortable sound of the engines lulled me back to sleep again.

Next thing I knew I woke up just in time for breakfast and I'd had a full tray of selection of foods. I ignored the sticky croissants, the marmalade, jams and honey and the toast in favour of my favourite cereal of which I got to choose from a selection of boxes. My favourite was the tiger one, "Rrrr," I'd said to myself I wish I'd slept through this and had it with a bit of milk. Afterward I tore my microwave meal of a fully cooked breakfast, with Linda McCartney sausages, open and ate with relish. Fully aware Jesus was watching I tried to eat delicately like a little lady and then he winked at me. "Morning my lovely." He'd said and my toes curled up.

"This is cheesey." I thought and wandered what Peter was up to and I knew he'd be as enthralled by this amount of wealth Jesus had. I mentally had to pinch myself and thought the day Peter and I had on elephants then the ensuing safari. I began to compare the two of them. Peter made me feel so achingly normal and protected by him as the most credible suitor I'd ever get to understand.

Jesus made me feel like I was worth a lot to him and was opening my eyes to a whole other world as I remembered my first flight over to Arabia with my family on a passenger plane with loads of other people. Mum told me beforehand that it was demanded we kept our anonymity all the way to Arabia. I thought Jesus's situation through rationally 'cause if the cat was truly out of the bag about Utopia school then Jesus was bound to show each of us girls what it would be like if we married him later on in life. I blushed again feeling wonderful that

I was chosen first. he must be approaching these arranged marriage suitors idea the same way I approached them, because I would have liked to take Peter first and probably would have made three trips that's all with Jesus second and a lad named Luke third 'cause this was the only lad eluding me for dates.

Coming back down to earth on the plane. I couldn't wait to get off it. The air was humid. The airport we landed in was really small and I noticed that we were near the edge of a cliff and Jesus told me to look down a shaft for us to climb in to. Now there was a helicopter there for tourists with a brilliant photographer in it. Jesus led me down this shaft on a really long ladder and then we jumped on the floor inside a really large cave. Then Jesus started to shake nervously and he asked for a cuddle. So I did and he started to make me have butterflies. I held on to him long enough to calm him down and I expected him to stick his tongue down my throat but he never. I don't know why he just did. Thankfully to spare my blushes we pulled apart in time to see Kara coming down and a professional rock climber who shouted up through the shaft, "It's all set up." While putting his thumbs up.

"Follow me," said the professional rock climber called Rick. We followed him for twenty minutes and there was a door and he said, "This is the back of Abraham Lincoln's face." We stepped through the door and three ropes with harnesses on dangled before us and Kara wanted to go first to test it and then gave thumbs up sign when she was attached. Jesus told me, "Remember to put your thumbs up when you're ready."

Jesus being Jesus said, "Now this is my first time doing this and I'm really nervous. Please give me another hug." So I cuddled him knowing full well I wouldn't show my fear and expected a kiss of gratitude which is what kept going through my head. "Why doesn't he kiss me?" 'Cause it was really obvious what he really wanted, but he wouldn't just take the lead. Then he pushed me forward to do it first and I felt elated thinking that he just wants me to go first at everything. It was brilliant after years of being the middle child after having to go second toffee over everything.

I soon got co-ordinated with my hands very well to get myself hooked up. Jesus on the other hand had fainted while I happily had my photo taken. It was amazing. he was winning me around slowly as I always felt the adventurer with him like the good old days of jumping off roundabouts in full rotations, and swings in mid-air.

When I came back in he was slumped by the wall with Kara holding out a cup of tea that one of the men, our personal body guard, came down with a flask. I stood there after I'd been given a cup of tea too and I'd bought a camera with myself but they said, "Put it away. It's not a touristic activity for just anyone and we know what picture you need to take next we'll take it for you."

"Yeah. I know." I blurted, "But I want everyone included in my photo, including the pilot, the two body guards, Rick the photographer and Kara."

"Right." Said Kara, "It was just going to be a picture of us three with Rick. Now who do you propose takes the photo of what you want to take?"

"Well George actually because I heard our pilot on the plane saying, "This is George taking over."

Everyone burst in to tears of laughter. "Uh…, yeah Karen we're taking the photos we want." Said Kara, looking embarrassed just to be with me. At least now Jesus was standing up looking puzzled but laughed with everyone else. At least he looked well and happy.

"Jesus I really wanted to practice my healing hands on."

"Where would you have put your hands on?" he said.

"Well on your head silly."

"Yeah. Knowing you, you would have done and you brighten up my day every time I do anything with you and yes," he'd said "I practice on the animals still do you."

"Well I can't master chasing the ducks yet. When all you did that day, in the park once, let us chase them to you, and you just scooped one up in your arms. Then we healed its little legs."

"I know." He said, "We're little healer people remember?"

"I know and I still want to be a vet, and I just worked out now what to do in the park if I want to pick up a lame duck to practice with my healing hands."

"Do you remember the guide in the aeroplane?"

I looked at Kara, "Well no. I was asleep most of the time."

"This place is Mount Rushmore in North Dakota. Do you remember the names of the other faces?"

"Oh, is it umm.., George Washington, Benjamin Franklin and John F Kennedy?" They just smiled at us they knew a ramble was coming on. "Or is it Jimmy Carter, no he's not famous, George W Bush senior, George Bush, or is it Margaret Thatcher on there or, is it…"

"Let me stop you right there. Now you obviously pay attention in class 'cause you seem to know a lot of Presidents of the United States. 'Cause I think you got it right the first time." The guide said, "Now why did you say Margaret Thatcher?"

"'Cause I was expecting everyone to laugh 'cause I'm getting used to people laughing at me on dates now. I really expected someone to jump in before and explain why they laughed about George. I also expected the guide to say you're right and Jesus to say you're amazing, but I never get the responses I want from people." And a little tear trickled down my face and thought "I've had enough of others making me feel stupid and start saying no to Jesus dates and try dating Matthew instead while still pursuing Luke. Someone has to click with me together 'cause mum always says that the right one will make you feel whole whenever you're together." It felt like Jesus wasn't really with me that day 'cause I expected some answers to come from his lips in more ways than one.

"Can someone tell me why you all laughed at the mention of George earlier?" Jesus asked on my behalf.

Kara answered, "It's the nickname given to autopilot which is a machine that can fly the plane for the pilot."

"Thank you Jesus." I said. "I wanted to ask but people like thinking I'm stupid."

"They do that to me too." and he hung his head looking shamefaced. "You're too good for me my Sherie Marie Kumar," he said softly, "This was supposed to have been a birthday treat and now I'm embarrassed to even look at you. Please give me a kiss and a cuddle."

"Sure I will. I thought you were going to give me a kiss earlier." And I puckered up with my eyes closed in anticipation, "I'm ready." I said.

"Oh get on with it." Said a bodyguard. So I hugged Jesus and he pecked me on the cheek.

CHAPTER FOUR

I blushed head to foot and thought, "Finally I've had a little kiss off one of my suitors. I hope I haven't made a baby." As if Jesus could read my thoughts he said. "Don't worry. You can't make a baby that way."

"Please tell me they're gonna teach us that in school instead of harping on about birds and bees. 'Cause my mum keeps on about true, true love makes babies and we really want you to find it here because we've ploughed too much money in to this."

"Right." The tower yelled, "We're going can you get on the plane please?"

I noticed little steps leading up to the entrance of the private jet.

"This has been fantastic!" I yelled out and I waved madly at everyone who helped make this day special. "Thanks everyone."

"Our pleasure."

On the plane we jetted off to Texas to see the Holy City. I stayed awake this time to make sure I heard our guide telling us what we were flying over encouraging me to look out over clear blue sky and I could see hundreds of buildings dotted around and famous landmarks. I was pleased that I'd had a kiss, my first ever kiss, from Jesus. It was all I could think about and it suddenly occurred to me. "I'll never have to get a paid job if I married you Jesus."

"But I thought we were going to be vets."

"Oh I know that. I meant that I could be bare foot and pregnant with you to be a mother with a large family. We could have eight children if we wanted."

"Do we have to talk about children?"

"But I've realised I only ever asked for a date from you once. When we had the picnic in the park. Do you love me?"

"Yeah I do." He said.

"Then say it." I'd said.

"No. I've been waiting for you to say it first."

Now being a blunderbust I said. "I love your dates. Can they all be like this?"

"What overly extravagant?" and I said "Yes. I'm aboard. I love you Jesus," and he still didn't say it. The tension hung in the air and I couldn't stop grinning.

"In thirty minutes we are set to land," said the pilot, so I kept staring out the window expecting a floating city in the sky as down below all I could see was lots of dry barren land.

"It's somewhere here right?" I asked Kara.

"I don't really know. I'd studied maps in anticipation but it wasn't anywhere on the ephemera. Now all Jesus is gonna say it's all about faith how you get to the real one but the make believe covered in jewels one is on a movie set in Texas. It will stay there forever they say as a tourist attraction."

I said, "Wey hey. I want to see the make believe one that's taken revelations far too literally."

"I know." Kara said, "But I'm more excited by seeing the real one that has the tree of life in and seeing the Red Amethyst Room."

"Oh that's right Jesus. You'd like a veterinary centre built there too wouldn't you? I remember that one."

"Kara. Have you ever seen one of our little miracles when we've healed with our hands little animals."

"I have." She said, "It's wonderful and kind. Kindness seeps out of your very beings. I'm sorry if we hurt your feelings earlier."

"It's ok. I'll learn to ask more questions and as I gazed out of the window a memory came to me of a date I went on once with a Jamie of where our chaperone Saint James said, "Already lead discussions with how, why, what, who, where and when. He'd been trying to help the shy group of children to interact intelligently." and thought that I'd have to apply those tactics with Jesus. I hoped we see the movie set version first in Texas.

The pilot said over the tannoy. "We're nearly there. I had my bible ready to be able to follow the guides tour of the site 'cause I'd had questions prepared I'd been writing down on the plan ready to ask the producer as I thought I might actually get to talk to famous actors and actresses 'cause I secretly wanted to get filmed.

"Now this is ridiculous you two," Kara said, "You're not talking much this trip."

So I said to Jesus, "You're making me nervous. I always expect you to take the lead." Then running at the bit I'd said. "Why do you ignore me Jesus?" and he said, "Wey hey, 'cause I can predict your personality 'cause you're very practical but willing to take risks with me so I assume you're going to take the lead with discussions sometimes."

"Did you learn that wey hey trick from one of St James lessons?"

"Oh. I'd forgotten that," he'd said, "It just comes automatically now. What have you been writing about?"

"Well I remembered writing down somewhere questions to ask a producer one day when I told the younger Jamie I'd like to be in movies one day."

"We're going to the real Holy City first mind."

"Right." I said, "I've just been day dreaming of walking on that movie set first."

"I haven't," he'd said.

"What were you thinking about when you fainted earlier? 'Cause I thought you were dreaming of angels willing to carry you outside of the mountain."

He'd said, "Actually yes. I've had nightmares of where I've been tempted to fly before by the devil himself."

"I didn't know you were scared of him."

"Well I am. I keep seeing in nightmares lately being tempted by Satan."

"It sounds like, to me," I'd said, "You're experiencing a type of regression in to a former life."

"What do you mean?" he asked innocently.

"Well it is possible that either you're experiencing what the real Jesus Christ went through thousands of years ago or you're really him re-incarnated."

"I didn't really follow that. But I am him, I keep hearing inside my head." I leaned over to give his hand a squeeze and looked directly into his eyes.

"I was thinking what your deepest fears might be."

"I love you." He said "I'm trying really hard to impress you. Nothing seems to faze you at all."

I blushed. I wanted to tell him something without hurting his feelings but just blurted it out anyway, "Don't you think we're a bit young for declaring our love for one another?" and he looked crushed ready to burst in to tears. I gave him a cuddle. "In a way I love you too as a friend. I'm nearly ten years old and I like dating other boys." Then I admitted, "But you're my favourite at the moment. Just give me a little kiss one in a while. A bit of French kissing as mum puts it. 'Cause I really liked your kiss on my cheek earlier and expecting an air kiss on the other side of my face earlier too."

"Air kisses?" Kara asked.

"Yes. Mum says it's a type of sophisticated kisses for little girls and boys usually done by French people or people in the theatre."

"Kiss me now," he said trying to take control by puffing out his little chest. I'd seen him do so man y times before when he'd got bolder enough to take the lead. I put my hands up into the air and leaned towards his face and kissed both cheeks. "That's what mum means."

"I'll do it to you now then." And he started to shake uncontrollably, Kara then interjected with tears of laughter streaming down her cheeks.

"It was a momentous occasion for me."

I'd said. "You're the first boy I'd ever French kissed before," and Jesus eyes lit up very happily.

"Really am I your first?"

I said, "Yes."

"'Cause I hear from older boys at school all the time saying they enjoy French kissing with their girlfriends and now I know what it is. I enjoyed that."

Kara still wanted to interject but her laughter stopped and then the bodyguards laugher stopped too. They realised that we'd both gone beetroot red all over as I hated being laughed at and then Jesus confessed that first. "I hate being laughed at," he said to the entire room on the plane just before we glided in to land. The pilot said, "Whoops. We've just bumped in to the roof of the real Holy City as it's still secretly being built or rather still under construction."

Everybody laughed then as it broke the tension. I was about to holler, "But there's not supposed to be a building in the Holy City," I'd said waving my bible about, "I've come with questions about that," I'd said, "and about this Red Amethyst Room."

Jesus and I were still huddling together just laughing nervously. Kara looked pitifully at us. "It's ok. That landing was a bit rough. I admit it. But we haven't landed on a sky scraper this time like we did before."

Mine and Jesus nervous laughter then abated and I smoothed down my long flowing garments as I'd changed after a wash on the plane. I noticed Jesus clothes and said, "You look very handsome today. This is the best fun I've ever had." I let out a huge sigh of relief and so did he. I smoothed down my dress again and re-adjusted my sari, which to me, was really just a sash according to other children. Perhaps I'd learned the wrong word for my wonderful colourful robes. I'd been told to put the colour orange on my forehead of which I did with an amber jewel just so that we could be formally introduced to the new founders of The Amethyst Rooms. Their surnames were Khan and Jesus said. "I've been rehearsing in my head. Good morning my name is Jesus and this is my girlfriend Sherie Marie Kumar and I now declare this building as open and fully ready for business. It was meant to be a surprise for you Sherie as the place is going to be where we'll work together side by side in years to come."

"Oh, so no-one else is going to get to do this with you?"

"Well no. You're my favourite suitor Sherie. It takes a lot of guts for me to be able to do this as this is my first official engagement. Thank you for coming with me. you never let me down Sherie Marie like the other girls do some times. Ssh." he said to me, "There it is over there. It's called the Jesus William veterinary surgery just for us. In the future dad says it's our destiny."

I beamed very privileged feeling yet again. "I've been and done so many firsts with you this weekend. It'll feel just like a dream when we get back. I've been writing in a book a diary every day of what I've been up to."

"I know," Jesus said, "All of us at the school has had to do that too. Am I still your favourite?"

"Right here. Right now. Yes." I'd said automatically. "But mum says I'm at an age when I can still keep my options open and I can't wait to share this with my friends back home in Pakistan and at the school of whom are Ruth and Rachel."

"Right." He said, "We are proving to father and the world that Utopia actually works and we are using the press here to write down what we want to tell everybody."

"Is there a Swing Set Park in the city?" I asked.

He said "Yes, but we got to do official things dad says on our own to feel our little wings. The appointment to cut the ribbon is this afternoon and please don't embarrass me."

"This is amazing," I said, "But I need some exercise from being stuck on planes and a helicopter."

"I understand." Said Kara, "It's part of the itinerary anyway. I'll take you there and I just have to add, you look very beautiful Sherie."

I said, "Thank you. I just..., I want to sit on some swings."

"It'll be this afternoon. Right after lunch we cut the tape. Jesus has to say a few words and we told you Sherie to keep your questions to a minimum because you need rhetorical questions for the press. We have a routine in our heads for you two idiots to perform in public."

"Now Sherie when I say press there will only be one journalist and one photographer so try not to be so nervous you two will be fine." She looked to me and said, "You'll have an opportunity later on to get changed into jeans for the park for opening time so that you and Jesus with other boys and girls can christen it."

In the afternoon after lunch and sprucing ourselves up we went to the new veterinary centre together to cut some tape like Kara said. There was a huge crowd waiting of adults with children.

Jesus had to stand on a podium and he said, "We welcome you all to introduce to you a new veterinary practice in the Holy City."

Then the journalist asked, "Why a veterinary practice?"

Then it was my turn. My tummy turned over with loads of butterflies and I said, "Why not a veterinary practice? It would be a strong message to the world that some very wealthy people in the world still actually care."

The journalist piped up, "This is my article, I'd like to ask the questions. How did you come to this idea?"

Jesus said, "My father did when I started to teach other boys and girls at Utopia school how to place healing hands on the animals."

"Wow," the journalist said, "Children can actually have a say in how things are run in this world."

"Can I interject?" I asked, "I need to explain don't I?" I looked to Jesus for support and he nodded his head as if to say, "Go on."

"That caring for others and proper integration of all races, colours, creeds and religions is necessary." I looked to Jesus again with pleading eyes.

"You're right Sherie. This is my girlfriend." He puffed out his chest "and we now declare this place open."

Someone gave him the biggest pair of scissors I'd ever seen so that he could cut some red ribbon in front of the door to the vets and I beamed up at him with pride. I knew that this took him a lot of guts to do and he cut it easily.

"We are now going over to the new Swing Set Park." My boyfriend said, "To cut some more ribbon." And his eyes twinkled at me.

I couldn't resist, "Happy birthday Jesus." I yelled. "Can we all sing happy birthday as he is ten years old today?" and all the adults started singing. I just couldn't resist mortifying him to everyone and I swelled with pride that we were really doing this.

On the way over to the park I asked the photographer if I could have a copy of his Polaroid pictures.

He said, "Yes."

I felt empowered, "Can we say let's cut the tape together Jesus?"

"I'd love to," he said "and we're sticking to the script."

"Now St James went through this with me. All we've got to really do is not say the first thing that pops into my head and say we now declare this open."

"Well yeah," Jesus said and he went to hold my hand. I saw him and knew I'd grab his hand wherever we went from now on. How could someone so unbelievably shy around girls pull of a wonderful weekend so easily and speak to a huge crowd of children following us with their parents to the local park. I spied a huge ribbon draped right round some railings encircling the whole of the swing sets with a huge bow over the gate.

"There's no scissors this time is there Kara?"

She said, "How do you know?"

"I guessed because I want Jesus and I to untie the ribbon at the bow by taking one end each."

She said, "That's a good idea." Of which we both did and declared the park open between us. "It's ok." Kara said, "I've got a pair of your jeans ready if you want to go to the ladies."

I was soon in and out and wished my friends and family were here to see this but I saw a BBC world wide van turn up as I went to have a slide and a huge camera followed Jesus around. I was jealous as I felt free to go on the swings next and blow off some steam for as long as I wanted.

I caught up with Jesus and Kara later when I came out of the park.

"At least the press are in the right place in the world now." Kara said to me.

"You're right this is a better way of dealing with them. To distract them to get to where we want them to be."

I beamed they made it sound like it was all my idea. This was wonderful. As we'd reconvened in the park our HRH helicopter showed up again to take us away from there to find the jewels encrusted Holy City movie set. The noise from the helicopter was horrendous but we were soon there and it looked amazing as we hovered over the top of it. They had no intention of landing but we were so low it looked fantastic. I looked over to Jesus.

"Don't worry about him he's just broken out in cold sweats." As Rick said to me. "We're off now to John F Kennedy airport. It'll be an hour's ride."

They said three days it had felt more like four by the time we reached Arabia's timeline and we had to put our clocks back.

I felt exhausted and was soon back in my home quarters. I started planning in my head a way of saying thank you by getting a big card for Kara and for Jesus and everyone else involved too. I made a list that said Mr and Mrs King of the Jews, Jesus, Kara and Rick and I thought that'll do as I left the list on my night stand before I drifted in to a very deep sleep and I dreamed of home in Pakistan. I thought wow this is so different. I wonder what the whole family would think of Sherie Marie Kumar of being on the front page of every magazine and newspaper I could think of and fell back to sleep again.

Mum came in with a cup of PG Tips in the morning with McVities chocolate hob nobs. then she let me go back to sleep. I heard her say to the family, "She's got jet lag. It'll take a couple of days until she can go back to school."

In my dreams I was flying over the jewel encrusted city again and thought I'd love to go back there to get an actual look around but they said that they had some trouble recently with jewels falling out of walls and we could have hurt ourselves which was what I'd worried about at the time when I first learned of the place in school.

I awoke again to some dinner and it was dark outside.

"Can I go back to school tomorrow?" I'd said to mum. "I've got a lot to talk about with my friends."

She looked me in the eye, "Not yet love. I had to sign a privacy agreement. There are certain things you are not allowed to talk about."

"Like what mum?" I felt indignant, "The whole world's press was there."

"I know, but Graham Oliver has insisted on this."

"Pah," I pouted, "I am not going to be one of Graham Oliver's disasters. I am not an idiot."

"Where did you pick that up from?"

"What?"

"Disrespect for the founder of this school."

"Oh. I think I heard it somewhere." I tried to rack my brains. There was always someone at school I had to protect but all I could think of was my teacher St James and I didn't know why. I wanted a date with Jamie Junior. I thought to myself but I also wanted a date with Luke. I was desperate to encounter what the fuss was all about. Then I thought who's James wasn't he the one with loads of ideas for the school. It's not him I thought. Then it clicked Jamie Junior must be Mr and Mrs Lloyds little boy who was a nuisance. I have to date him, but I can't remember why. all I can recall from Kara is that I keep getting my satirical sense of humour wrong to be compatible with little Jamie.

Now it was my birthday coming up and I decided to have a theme of princesses. I loved the idea of being Princess Jasmine and of dressing in her favourite pale blue outfit that was like a boob tube at the top and nice floaty trousers. Mum was going to have to take some convincing and I wanted all my class to be at my party. It was going to be that Saturday so after school one day I sauntered through the Swing Set Park and smiled to myself with a bit of pocket money on me. I stared at the others having a swing, sliding down the slides, and having a go on the roundabouts. The coiled animals had a child on everyone and I blushed thinking I want the children at my party to be that happy.

I sauntered through it all to down in the town and I came across a Martin's newsagents of where I stocked upon tiny little treats for party bags and a couple of banners and two bags of balloons. Then I found a Disney shop and I got Eve her Aurora dress, Fee her Snow White dress and my Jasmine's outfit. I then went over to the ethnic jewellery stand to get a jangly headdress for my Jasmine's outfit, a tiara for Eve's outfit and a black wig for Fiona. I'd been really pleased with myself but realised I had a lot to carry of which I didn't mind. Mum called me a little lady and little ladies should be allowed to get on with things mum says. I hugged all my bags to myself and was secretly smiling as I walked back through the Swing Set Park of where I met up with Luke with all the girls around him. I managed to catch his eye and he ran over to me and said. "Can I help you with your bags?"

I blushed wondering why he was being so nice but I said, "Thank you. I've been trying to get a date with you for ages."

"Wow." He said. "A girl who's asked me out for a change."

"But I've been trying to secure a date with you for ages through your chaperone Kara. She's my chaperone too."

"But all you had to do was ask me." He said.

"Well talk about invitations did you receive my mum's for my birthday party?"

"I didn't see it," he said, "But mum did say I had a party to go to this weekend."

"That's my birthday party," I'd said. "I'm eleven this Saturday."

"That's brilliant," he said, "Now I know who mum's getting a present for."

"Oh I know isn't it annoying when mums get other people's presents for you."

"Actually I enjoy it. How's Ruth and Rachel by the way?"

"Annoying as ever. Last time I saw them they were arguing about you. I haven't worked out why yet."

"Does it matter?" he winked at me. "I arrange all my dates and I'll date who I want to date. I wanna date you 'cause I know the others argue about me. That's what I was doing with the other girls trying to sort their arguments out and I'm sick of them arguing over me."

"How many have you been out with?"

"Well that's the thing I set my cap at older girls and your friends think I'm more mature than the other boys and fight over me and I love it. It makes me feel more popular with the girls. Is this where you live?" He asked with two bags in his arms, as we walked into my hallway. "Shall I put them here?"

"No thanks. I'm keeping them upstairs till tomorrow."

"I could come round early tomorrow if you want and help you set up for your party."

"Why thank you. It's supposed to start at two o'clock. Say I'll see you at 1pm?"

"That's fine. I'm dating Rachel tonight so I'll see you tomorrow."

I thought great I'll see what he's like with Rachel and perhaps get to know him as a friend. I then went downstairs after we'd dumped our bags of where I'd said to my mum. "I'm having a shower for tonight now mum and I'm going to hog the bathroom for an hour."

"Not too long mind 'cause the whole family can't wait to jump in too." Said mum. "Hurry up yeah. Your sisters have got dates."

"Ok. That's fine." I said and was soon lathering myself up with what I was going to wear through my mind. It had to be a traditional brightly coloured dress. I couldn't wait to go on this date. I told St James I'd look after his little boy of whom I pointed out to him. "Look I know he's your son so I'll ask Kara to come with us too and so you can keep an eye on little Jamie and not worry. I'll take good care of him," as I asked Kara for advice of what Jamie Junior liked.

She then asked me, "Wouldn't you like to go off with both his parents?" This old conversation was going through my head in the shower as this happened mid-week last week.

"I'd love to meet Mr and Mrs Lloyd." I'd said. Then I stepped out of the shower and accepted a towel from a maid and dried myself. I started humming my favourite tune from Madame Butterfly and wanted to look my best. Jamie could be a new friend and I can use the ruse of chaperones for dates for going out to places I'd love to go to until I'm married to Jesus. Mum said she was always happiest with our dates.

CHAPTER FIVE

That evening we sat in our boxes looking down over the stage. I felt every surge of emotion going through to my very soul every time they sang, danced and acted and Jamie put his arm around me as I let a little tear run down my cheek.

"You smell nice," he said, "What perfume is that?"

"Mmm." I was only half listening. "Pagan." I said getting carried away with what was on the stage and Jamie's arm felt warm and familiar like I was getting a hug from my brother. I wanted to talk to him afterward but then there came an interlude. The play taught me something about deep emotions and reminded me of how vulnerable the Lloyds lad was. I turned round to Jamie after batting his arm away and said. "Look don't get the wrong idea about me I am not looking for love with you. In fact I'm using you to go and see different things I haven't experienced before."

His dad and mum sat behind us. "Thanks for the honesty. He does wear his heart on his sleeve." Karen said. "You just want a friendship don't you?"

"Well I make better friends this way." I said. "Otherwise I get lonely. My two best friends are Ruth and Rachel. Can I date my girlfriends? They're always on about wealth and I say 'What knowledge?' and they say' No money'."

"But I want to learn and gain a lot of knowledge and experience. Mum tells me that in the end we all get our one, one true love anyway so I just make the best of things. I really miss my friends in Pakistan and being able to go back to my roots and speak my own language. I miss my cousins and their children and my uncle and aunty."

"It's ok." Karen said, "Don't ever lead our little boy on will you?"

"It's ok mum. I talk to other children all the time and arrange my own dates too Sherie but I ask the girls in question to set me up with my family around."

"Now I appreciate your honesty." The dad said. "He'd make a good friend you know. You're a lovely little girl. Have you got a favourite at the moment, 'cause that may change later on."

"I know and I really like Jesus, and Peter and I'm getting to know Luke."

"Talk to me mum, please why do I have to ask you to set me up on dates?" said Jamie, "When my own father is my personal chaperone."

"Well how else are we going to get dates without having to get parental approval?" I said.

"You can't." Jamie said as we walked hand in hand quietly with his family around us.

"What's your sisters' name Jamie?"

"It's Corinne."

"And your parents are Karen and James?"

"Well yeah."

It was a nice easy silence as we walked back home to our quarters.

"I'm going home soon back to Pakistan for a holiday."

"That's nice. You're so beautiful," he said. That made me blush and him blush too.

"I like you." I said as I turned to him to look him in the eye. "Have you had fun tonight? 'Cause for me it was amazing as mum always said to me 'It'll either call to your very soul or over time you learn to appreciate if even if you don't like it very much'."

"I really like it Sherie. Do you want to give me a kiss?"

"Oh I'm saving those mums says kisses make babies."

Hand in hand it was a nice walk home out under the stars. I loved the atmosphere and the night time felt so cool which was nicer than the searing heat through the day time.

At my door I asked him if he wanted to come to my eleventh party and he said, "Yes I'd love to. Are my parents going to have to come?"

"You'll have to ask them. I ask my parents and chaperone Kara for everything."

"I want to be on my own tomorrow."

"What free from dates?"

"Well yeah. I want a little kiss."

"Mum says you can't hurry love. It just sort of happens." Next thing I knew he lunged into me for a kiss. It was wet and soppy. I wiped my mouth, "Ummm. That was nice." He said and I hurried in doors.

"Good night Jamie. I'll see you at my birthday." It was so late and I leaned against the front door as I did a lot after dates and thought about my family back home. My goals in life were finding a husband, making the most out of school as I really wanted to be a vet. Then Jesus's face floated before my eyes. We said we'd do university together and be best, best friends forever. That lad made me think of Rachel and Ruth's constant dilemma of whom was the hottest, or the coolest boy they ever dated and all their arguments seemed to rest on Luke. I don't think Jamie understood me very well. Jesus, well I didn't have to ask for dates most of the time and Peter made me feel comfortable with him. I really did fancy both of them but when I thought about everything Jesus and I did together it was always completely over the top, but his lifestyle is amazing. Mum told me to watch him he's getting carried away with you. I thought of that kiss with Jamie. According to my friends they made a list in their heads of whom could give them the best kiss out of ten. That was a definite three I thought but I had no-one to compare it with. I loved the way Jesus blew me off my feet. He was the kindest healer of the animals out of all of them. Peter had the way of making me worry, 'cause if I'd had that safari trip as a date with Jesus I wouldn't have been so scared. He totally made me feel empowered. That was brilliant on our dates and I wrote all this down in my diary mum said it would help me to think. I just need to talk with boys more at school and just try to make friends with them. Luke's way of thinking about older girls made me wonder should I try an older student as a suitor. I yawned. I needed a rethink on these date scenarios and went to bed. I had another problem to a hairy one. I was beginning to get a black haired moustache and my legs and arm pits were doing that too. My periods had recently started and at least I had a waxing session in the morning before my party. I wanted to knock them dead. I floated from the bathroom after brushing my long dark hair out a hundred times as my favourite servant Lucy used to like to do when I was younger. I am getting more grown up now and was determined to make others believe I could do things on my own. Then the hired help would give me space to breathe. I fell in to bed in my favourite blue night dress hugging my favourite blue teddy bear. My friendship with Ruth and Rachel had taken a back burner these days so I'll have to go out with Luke just so that I could talk about the same things they did.

In the morning Lucy drew me a bath and I climbed in up the marbled steps. "Lucy."

"Yes."

"Would you mind if I drew my own baths in the morning?" she blushed and looked uncomfortable.

"Why Sherie? I am paid to do this."

"I know but I feel like I'm behind the times with my friends and I need to grow up. Take control and give myself more responsibilities." Then it hit me. I had fun with Jesus opening up new buildings. I wondered what other social engagements he got involved in outside school. "I'd like to do more of that." I said to myself. "I'll help in those social obligations with him I'd say at my coming of age party." I just floated in the bath for ages just thinking and wondered at Karen and James, mum and dad, and Mr and Mrs King of the Jews relationships. Would I have a same equal partnership with Jesus one day? I could get involved in politics back in Pakistan to show him I have a voice on certain subjects. I grabbed my scratcher and began talking to it pretending I was being interviewed.

"Now Miss Kumar pleased to meet you."

"Pleased to meet you too." And I'd shake their hands and tell them all about the plight of animals being pushed to the brink of extinction. This was to be my cause. Then I thought of my favourite prayers to Mecca and wandered if I could teach my friends to sing it the same way I do. I've always been proud of my heritage.

I got out of the bath singing in Urdu my favourite rock song from Asian radio I could find on my digital tv in my bedroom. I listened to that song to get me in the mood for my birthday. I got my prayer pillow in front of the window and made a point of leading my favourite with Lord I ask of you that my party goes well today. Mohammed's visit really shook me up that time. I was actually scared of him the founder of my faith would have a go at me if I got this wrong.

Afterwards I went through my favourite classical music and asked mum, "What would you rather have classical or rock music for my birthday?"

"A bit of both love not all of us adults can put up with that rock rubbish you listen to but I realise it's your birthday."

"Yeah but mum I like Ghazai classical music very much but none of my friends would dance to it."

"You'll be surprised sweetheart at how many would dance to that. Me and your dad would."

"Mum can I stay up later tonight to watch something called The Sketches Musical?"

"Of course you can it's Sunday tomorrow."

"I want to lead prayers later at my party with everyone leading my favourite Meccan prayer."

"Yeah you drive us to distraction with that one five times a day every Saturday."

"But the boys who work on our favourite radio show tell us to do it that way on Pakistan FM."

I then found my sari and put on long flowing brightly coloured garments and said to mum. "Are you still coming with me to get waxed?"

"Of course I'm coming. Wild horses wouldn't drag me away from enjoying this special day with you."

"Let's get going then. I'm eager to show Peter and Jesus that I'm all grown up and I'm putting on make-up later. I want one of them to say I'm beautiful."

"You do look beautiful sweetheart. I wonder what your sisters are wearing."

"We'll find out later but we'd better go. I don't want to be late mum."

"Ok." Then we jumped into our Chevrolet and headed for the beauticians. mum had arranged for all four of us a waxing session. All you had to do was strip to get our legs done and under the arms. Mum and I were the only ones to get our moustaches off. For me that really stung. They put on a heap of moisturisers afterwards and I felt lovely, like a little princess and then we all had make-up put on to compliment our skin tones and I got talking to the beauticians for ages. I put my favourite party dress on and the dot in the middle of my forehead was orange.

"That's better isn't it?" said mum, "Now we can all feel like proper princesses."

"Yes." They said.

I was inwardly looking forward to how many would turn up to my little party as all the children in my year at school had been invited.

Tap, tap the door went and I adjusted my beautiful long hair that mum had insisted on leaving it looking natural. I was always more beautiful mum said with my hair down. I wondered if I looked old enough for Luke to see if he'd ask me out. Mum said that I'd actually got pulling power now. I'd even had my first bra today that I'd felt the need to stuff. I wanted to get kisses today to mark them out of ten. I'd try it Ruth and Rachel's way and lo and behold it was them at the door with arms full of presents. I was dead keen to open them but mum told me to wait until they'd all gone home so I said quite politely, "Could you please put them on our hallway table."

Which they did and upon eyeing them up I guessed which presents they'd bought off my list I'd sent out with my invitations.

"Come on in." my mum said from the living room. Then Luke turned up with his friends and Kara looking very beautiful not what she would wear at all while chaperoning.

"Wow. You look stunning." Luke said.

"Do you think I'm old enough for you now?" It came out seductive like I planned. I just wanted to hear Peter and Jesus reactions too. I wanted to try out a new line with Jesus as he came in and lo and behold Jesus was at the door and his eyes were gleaming at me.

"What do you think Jesus do you like me?" and I did a little twirl that I'd learned at ballet.

"Beautiful." he said looking appreciatively and I wanted to kiss him so I asked him.

"Do you want to kiss me?" and I gave a little girlie giggle. He laughed, "Beautiful." He said again. Then Peter turned up and I had a better routine for him.

"How do you do, you're pleased," I made eyebrow movements before I'd said, "to meet me."

"Yes." He said "You look beautiful." I blushed and twirled my hair seductively. He leaned in and asked me if I'd had his present yet.

"No." The table at this point was crammed with presents. I really wanted a boy to kiss me to find out what the fuss was all about between Ruth and Rachel. Luke came in next and said, "Wow. Who looks older tonight?" and he did the eyebrow thing. "I could fancy you."

I blushed again this was going all wrong. I had to greet everyone at the door mum said. Deep down I ended up looking forward to Christmas to try the mistletoe routine the girls had giggled about after last year's party held at the grand hall at our school.

The last one in was little Jamie and he said to me. "Can I have a little kiss?"

My immediate reaction was to say no but I offered up my cheeks like the French do. I pointed to my cheeks and said, "Here." And I started walking backwards in to the party room where everyone could see him kissing to get someone jealous enough to actually want to kiss me like Jamie did and he kissed my cheeks. It was still a four out of ten. I desperately wanted to test out Peter's, Jesus, and Luke's kisses.

Several girlfriends turned up then and I turned on some Urdish music and tried to convince everyone to sit on cushions so I could teach them my favourite Meccan prayer and told everyone to look to the east outside the living room window. I desperately wanted to pray to Allah but I knew I wasn't allowed and every attempt to pray came out as "Abba father."

I got there in the end though as my girls did me proud and I thought I'd heard it properly coming from Jesus. I felt elated with my Urdu music as everyone got up to dance. This was my turn to shine. I'd said to myself and enjoyed the best birthday ever but I only ended up getting kisses from my parents as they both said, "We're really proud of you."

"Mum. Will my seduction techniques ever work?"

"I don't know darling. Keep trying. You've tried with your father enough."

"Yeah and every time I'd tried something different on him he said yes I know those boys it might work and I'd said thanks dad."

I went to bed that night really happy in some ways but a bit miffed. I wanted to have experience with kissing.

Now in the morning after a nice bath I combed my hair about one hundred times and got ready to go to my Mosque with my family and Jesus turned up with his mum and dad and his siblings. Ahmed and Sara were beaming next to my dad and they started talking about babies and I said. "How many times did you kiss to create a baby?"

Sara piped up, "Too many times to count," and Ahmed pulled her to him and they shared a little kiss and I impertinently asked. "Are you pregnant?"

"Well yeah." Sarah said. "The baby is due mid-February and we can't wait."

"Well congratulations. Let's go and pray." Which they did all together with everyone else in lines in front of the preacher.

This turned out to be a lovely weekend as when I went outside of the Mosque afterward Jesus said to me, "I think I love you." This completely floored me and all I could say was, "Thank you. No. I mean I think I love you too."

"I love the way you stay rooted in your faith and the fact you're teaching me about how you think." I smiled up at him as he was a little bit taller and he kissed me. I got a little zing through my body down to my toes. "Wow!" I thought this is a ten out of ten and went and smiled all day long after I found myself asking for another date.

"I hoped you'd do that," said Mary his mum, "Jesus told us all that happened yesterday."

"Where would you like to go next?"

I said, "Home to Pakistan. I could show you off to my cousins."

"We'll arrange it." Said Mary. "It's a date."

The next day was the last day of school before we started having lessons outside the class and was the last week before half term. "Can we have the date during half term?"

"Yes Sherie that is our way of thinking." Peter looked across at us and I thought he looked jealous. He must have seen us kiss so I walked over to him.

"I think we'd better start seeing each other as friends." And he grabbed my waist and pulled me in for a kiss that took my breath away and I thought I was going to faint. A definite nine and a half out of ten as my knees went weak and I thought that I was going to fall over. I put this all in my journal.

The next day we had rounders and I wanted to choose my team. I'd chosen Andrew, John, Mark, Luke and Jesus and the girls were Ruth and Rachel, Esther and Mary for my team. I got them to let me flip the coin. "Heads we go first." I shouted and flicked the coin into the air perfectly to land in my other hand of which I covered and showed it to Jamie. "It's tails," the teacher said, "Do you want to bat first Jamie?" He'd said, "Bat." So I led my team to spread out around the field.

The game started and Jamie hit the ball really hard straight at Ruth and I spied a man at the edge of the playing fields with a large expensive camera.

"Wait a minute!" I shouted and got Miss Jackson. "There's a man over there who shouldn't be here," and I saw her squint in to the sun of where I'd pointed. He was still there.

"Thank you for telling me," and she got out her mobile phone and heard her talk to security. "Carry on playing. Security will sort him out."

It was a long game and I worried the whole time and saw a security man all in black step forward to deal with him then other help from men in black grabbed his arms to escort him from the school grounds.

Now I knew this was going to make the press tomorrow and freaked out. All our lessons this week were supposed to be outside. These tourists. It had to be tourists. I reasoned inside of my head we're all ways going to turn up and I thought I'd put my neck on the line to help with publicising the school. The magazine was simply called Utopia and I wanted to get involved.

Now it was my team left to bat and my arm still played up occasionally as it really twinged. I thought we'd deterred the press away from the place. I soon got myself out as I couldn't bear the twinge in my shoulder and walked over to the other children in the field playing rounders too and told their teacher James what was going on.

Now St James had always seen this coming. He said to me. "It's not tourists. It's the press. Could you put up with it Sherie, later on in life if you married Jesus?"

"I don't understand. I thought this school had its own publicity machine anyway that sold to the rest of the world."

"look I am St James. I've been warning Mr and Mrs King of the Jews about this happening. Nobody listens to me. Now go back to your classroom they've all gone inside."

"Yes sir." I'd said politely and bowed to him. I'd been wanting to speak to him about satirical as mum kept telling me that I was getting it all wrong. I stayed there though to ask him if I could help on the schools magazine with little Jamie. He told me to ask him myself.

"Is he going to keep asking me for a kiss?"

"No." he said. "Go back to your classroom." And I blushed again, "I'm sorry sir. I'm going," and I did. I realised things were going to change at our brilliant school and I wanted to fully be involved and help the school out. I couldn't wait for my holiday next week. I was going to see Moneesha and Neesha my father's sisters children as well as all my other cousins, Rhaja, Joni and Maahem my mother's sisters children.

During lunch time I went to the schools press office and asked Suzy if I could help. She said, "Yes, but wouldn't you want to work on the schools magazine?"

"Well I do. This is the schools press office isn't it?"

"One day you can get involved here if you want to and I love your gumption but the school magazine runs in the English department."

I moaned in Urdu. I didn't want to upset Suzy. "Right. In the English block three doors down it say quite plainly Utopia magazine, editor in chief is Jamie Junior."

"Ok." I said, "Thank you." And I bit my lip and my stomach growled so I took my lunch box back to the canteen and found my friends Ruth and Rachel of whom I sat with and nibbled on my samosa, before attacking my crisps and choccy bar. I also had a nice Granny Smith's apple.

"I'm going to work on the schools magazine." I'd said to my friends.

"Why have you asked Jamie and his father?"

I said "Yes. Well at least…, I mean I've already asked St James."

"Go to the office now," said Rachel, "Didn't you get a straight A during our last S.A.T.s?"

"Well yeah. I'd make a good reporter." I repeated that sentence in my head over and over again as I made my way to the office. I only had twenty minutes before next class.

I banged on the door loudly.

"Come in," Jamie said and I stopped short when I saw a lot of pictures on the wall, and recognised a lot of pictures of Jesus and boys and girls holding medals and cups. I blurted out, "How come I'm not up there I'm forever getting A's?"

"I know we could put you on the high achievers list, sometimes we already do. You're in this week's edition."

"But I never said you could put me in."

"Yes you did. At the beginning of school everyone's parents sign a form saying that I could publicise your names and take photos. Obviously your parents had said yes. Let me show you something."

"Ok." Jamie was having me at a loss for words.

"Here are the last three months negative and you and Jesus are near the top. Have a look."

It was us alright. Me on Mount Rushmore, and Jesus and I opening the new vets in America and the new Swing Set playground. "It's not as good as ours is it?" I told him.

"I know. Why are you here?"

"Ummm," completely flummoxed I tried hard to remember the line I was going to use. I cleared my throat. "Can I work on the magazine please?"

"What would you write about?"

"Well I'd like a column every week."

"About what?"

"How the dating machine works around here 'cause I think it's brilliant." I saw his face as about he'd like to say something and I got closer to him and said with my finger in the air.

"Now let me finish." He said.

"Now the way in which I date and the perfect arranged marriage scenarios are the best aspect of the school. One column please to promote what we should openly be proud of and I'm calling Sherie in the Utopia city with the by-line of This Is How We should Date."

"Look where is this going to 'cause it could turn in to a whose dating whom article."

"But it won't. I'm writing about myself and how the dating system outside of school should work. I don't want to bring the school into disrepute. Now let me finish. There was a photographer that the security guards had to throw out today."

"This magazine covers every aspect of this school."

"Can I please have a column depicting my point of view. The line could read how to survive dating at Utopia."

"Right ok." He said. "That's fine. Give me a blue print copy and I'll add it in."

"Thank you. I could kiss you, but I won't, but I need to try something and I leaned in for a kiss on the lips.

"Wow," he'd said, "You're very forward. I'm determined to find my ten out of ten kisses."

"Well how was that for you?"

"It was wonderful ten out of ten. How was it for you?"

"A bit wet and sloppy about four out of ten."

"I'll keep looking then, but I won't be here during summer months as my mum and dad are taking me to France."

CHAPTER SIX

At fifteen years old I was well established as a Dear Deirdre, my mum said after people got bored of hearing about my dating and my quest to find one true love 'cause I thought that was what the school was about. I was still getting straight A's for everything and loved being with my boyfriend Jesus. Mum and dad were forever saying how proud they were of me. I enjoyed school so much and every year Jesus and I would go to Pakistan on his private jet to see my family and this year I'd seen a musical called The Sketches that was fantastic.

On mine and Peter's dates we went to the movies a lot and he still blew my mind away but was secretly in love with Jesus who'd still do expensive dates with me. Like during last summer after going to Pakistan they took me and my family to Canada to see more relatives and Niagara Falls. I had amazing times with Jesus and he never ceased to surprise me. I really enjoyed his company and loved his kisses that spine tingled me. Those kisses could last forever.

I found myself constantly arguing with my sisters over Peter who took them on better dates like to Verona in Italy and San Francisco in America. I grew jealous of my sisters as they were growing close to Peter and I couldn't get out of cinema date mode with him. I wasn't thick all he ever wanted to do was sit in the back row for a kiss and a cuddle.

Now Jamie still loved France and asked me several times if I'd go with him just as a friend. I really liked Jamie he turned out to be a good laugh and I found over the years we shared the same satirical humour. That I really liked. I was tempted to go with him this year as I'd never been up the Eiffel Tower before and fancied myself as shit hot with my French. I'd have loved to test this out in France so this year I said "Yes, I'd love to." Jamie was surprised.

"I could just see you on a bicycle with a wicker basket on the front selling baguettes and with garlic and onions strung round your neck. With a little red neckerchief on over a navy blue and white lined top with a kickee beret on your head." and he laughed. "I'd like to see your bare shouldered more and some make-up on your face."

"But I've always put make-up on. I like the natural look from my cosmetics."

"I didn't know, but I'd really like your company." And we went with his dad on our own.

On the plan Jamie could hold a really good conversation and we talked in Urdu and we spoke for ages and I really liked him. He had grown on me throughout the years of working on the school's magazine together. We gossiped and did a crossword together. We made each other laugh. He'd always been the class clown who'd always made everybody laugh.

The first day there we went to a little café and I had some croissants so did Jamie and his dad. We sipped wine together no-one suspected our ages and as people walked by Jamie would say. "Ooh, la, la," at good looking women and I did the same with handsome men to wind each other up. The drink flowed and we fell of the chairs giggling our heads off.

"Give me a kiss," he'd said.

"Go on then."

"No."

"I dare you."

"Am I still four out of ten?"

"No," and he kissed me, "You're now five out of ten but you're getting there."

"Who's the hottest now?" he said, and I hiccupped, "It has to be Jesus."

"And who's ninety-nine percent there?"

"It's gotta be Peter, but I am sick and tired of going to Utopia's cinema complex. I think he's getting fed up too 'cause I mainly ask for Bollywood films and he's sick of reading all the subtitles."

"At least I know Urdu."

"Well yeah." I'd said, "I wish he'd make more of an effort too."

"Who's the best at your Meccan prayer these days?"

"Oh, it's got to be us women and Jesus definitely wails louder than anyone else as he took me to the Wailing Wall once. I innocently thought that at eleven that there were speakers making the wall sound like it was speaking, I was glad Jesus took me there though to create a miracle as all the camels passed out in the heat. Him and I nurtured them back to health again."

"Oh, that's right you always wanted to be vets you two."

"Yes, it's true. Will you marry me?"

"No."

"Why not?"

"I don't love you like that."

"Like what?"

"Well. That I need you. I want to find a French bride."

"I'll put your lonely hearts ad in the Louvre on the wall."

"What's the Louvre?"

"It's a museum. Can you still do great graphics?"

"Uh yep. you need a bare chested photograph of yourself."

"I know. You're embarrassing me."

"Oh and show your face or you could be anyone. I'll tell you what I'd get an artist, like that one over there to do a painting of yourself. Now take off your top."

"Yep. I'll do that. Would you take yours off?"

"No."

"Why not? It's only a sash and I'm dreaming of your body."

"Now no means no in any language."

"Bon nuit," Jamie said.

"Bonn soir," I said, "Where are we going to?"

"Home Sherie. Can I call you Sher?"

"Only if you pose for the artist."

He said, "Yes. Do I need to buy a stripy top?"

"Not if you don't want to." And I laughed again. I loved to dare him to do things whenever we got drunk together. "Where's your dad gone anyway?"

"I dunno. Mum and dad left ages ago."

"But they're there."

"Where?" he said.

"There." I said, "Right behind you."

"Promise me you'll love me forever."

"'Cause I will you daft amos, best, best friends last forever."

"Was I ever lover material?"

"No. I only love you as a friend."

"You say that every time we're together, but you're right about my kisses aren't you?"

"Yep it's gone up to five out of ten."

"Who's ten out of ten?"

"It had to be Jesus."

"Yep. I knew you'd say that."

"Let's amble back home. I think we've got through two bottles of wine."

"I think we have." Then I shivered in the cold evening air and I put a shawl on.

"I could have put my coat on you and take you back to the hotel."

"Are you still trying to have your wicked way with me?"

"No. Jesus is my best friend but I am still going to be your best, best friend forever."

I looked towards a waiter and said, "Je voudrais du vin s'il vous plait?"

"What's your favourite?"

"Sauvignon blanc."

"We'll have it and take the bottle back to the hotel."

"Stop tickling my neck." I said. "I don't like it."

"I know but I can't help it. My last girlfriend said I had spaghetti arms."

"Did you rate her out of ten?"

"Yep, she was a seven."

"I'm so glad I got to know you. Where's your parents? I need St James chaperoning."

"Of course you do," he said and we stumbled in through the entrance doors and tried very hard to be quiet as we got into the lift.

"What number are we?"

"I don't know, try number five, room 108."

"I love our friendship." I'd said and leaned in with a soppy kiss.

"Ugh," he said. "That's too wet."

"Oh sorry. I just fell on your lips."

"You're right." And we giggled. "I want to finish this new bottle of wine."

"Well yeah. We're just a couple of winos really."

"I've had bestest laughs with you Sherie ever."

"I need to give Jesus a call on +60 01749 832436."

"You are all right?" Jesus said as I'd dialled his number.

"I'm just a little bit drunk with my best, best made Jamie."

"Fine. Can we have a date?"

"Yep. Where to? It's Canada you wanna take me to isn't it?"

"Well yeah."

Then Jamie breathed down my neck. "I want to go there too."

"Maybe you'll find someone in France. My Sherie is great as a fixer upper mate."

"I don't need you to do this for me," said Jamie, "I want you Karen," he'd said to his mum. "Will you set me up on a date with Fiona?"

"What Sherie's sister?"

"Yep. Though I want to find a blonde bombshell who's French by the way."

"Well maybe when you're sober tomorrow my sister could wow you with her A-level French over the phone or I could set you up for real."

"Ah. A date. A proper one at last. I want a blonde bombshell. I used to think they were women with bombs."

"You've always made me laugh," I'd said, "I'll say goodnight to Jesus when I'm in my room. Jamie swayed slightly and then puked all over my shoes. The sight and smell made me urge all over his shoulder as we bumped heads.

"Right where's my room?" he said.

"Over there. To the left there's 108 and I sleep in here 109 just opposite."

"Good night then." He'd said.

"God bless." I'd said.

"I love you." He'd said, "I might find a future wife in Fiona. When are you going to Canada?"

"The last week in August."

"Just before school starts?"

"Well yeah."

"Have a nice time."

"Look I need to go in my room and put these clothes in a bag for the hotel laundry service. Swill my mouth out and clean my teeth before I put on my pyjamas."

"Come in to my room anyway after you've cleaned up and get into your pyjamas Sherie. Will you marry me?"

"No." I'd said, "I want to get clean. What do you want me in your room for afterwards?"

"Nothing. I love being with you. Go your own way though you always do." Jamie said and he let himself in to his room. I got in mine but soon got myself sorted and jumped into bed and my head swam for ages. It felt like I was on a boat and fell asleep.

In the morning I got up with a banging headache and room service hanged on the door.

"It's outside."

"What?"

"My laundry. Then I spied it by the wardrobe and let the maid in. I tipped her ten francs and said, "Thank you." and let her go on her way. Sat at the dressing table I spent ages on my hair after I dried it."

There was a knock on the door.

"Oh go away room service will you my heads banging," and Jamie crept in and made me jump out of my skin.

"Coming down for breakfast?"

"How come you're so perky?" I asked. "I was secretly hoping you were feeling ill too."

"Ah not me. I can hold my drink. Do it with me my baby."

"No. I am a virgin and I intend to stay that way."

"I'd like you to go up the Eiffel Tower today with us."

"Sounds like fun," and I swayed around on the dressing table stool nearly collapsing. It was my first time with Jamie sipping wine. I didn't know that it would go straight to my head.

"How are you so perky?" I asked Jamie and wondered how on earth I ended up here. I was really missing Jesus as I paraded round in my birthday suit. "Sit on the bed if you want Jamie while I get dressed." Now Jamie had an eyeful and I didn't care. He was my mate. I crawled my way to the bathroom. "I might be in here for an hour mate trying to sober up." I still felt drunk. There was a knock on the door, "Morning call eight o'clock."

It made me jump and I decided on jeans and a warm long sleeved t-shirt. I put on my make-up and my orange dot on my forehead and chose my favourite blue sash to go over my shoulder.

"I know not how to seduce you." Jamie pleaded.

"I don't want you to. You've been taking the piss since my birthday four years ago." My head was pounding. "Can you pick up my alka-seltzers? Please."

"Where are they?"

"In my vanity case on the bed."

He said, Weh hey! I've seen your body today and you're shit hot."

I said. "Thank you," and I sounded woozy when I said "Jesus has seen this a thousand times."

"No. he hasn't." and I grinned gripping everything insight trying to stabilise myself. Then picked up my glass of water with my alka-seltzers in, gave it a little twirl for the soluble to dissipate in to the water.

"Aah. That felt nice." He sat there talking to me and waiting for me to move.

"Move your ass," he said, "We're going in five minutes."

"Nearly there with my make-up and I'm tying my long black hair out a minute."

Just outside the hotel we wandered across the grass towards the tower. We got in a lift for forty francs each and it took us straight to the top. I hung over the edge not able to work it out if it was the drink from the night before making me sway or was it vertigo but I wasn't scared. Where were the guide ropes and the harnesses? I asked myself.

"Grab my hand Sherie. I think you're going to fall over the side."

"But with you Jamie I became a risk taker."

"I know, but there's no ropes and I want to kiss you."

"If you do that I'll be sick."

"Just what I want to hear," he said sarcastically. It wasn't long until we went back down in the lift. At the bottom I felt relieved and released my breakfast. I was having a terrible time. I really wished I hadn't drunk so much wine.

Two days later we were coming home and Jesus came to meet me at the airport with a bunch of flowers and I ran straight over to him and said, "These carnations and roses look beautiful."

"Can I take you to tea tonight?"

"I really want to. In fact I'd love it. Where are you thinking of going to?"

"Perhaps Rome for tea and a nice two days away. Don't bother packing but come with me now. the holiday's already been booked. Do not worry we'll make it back in time for school."

"Sorry I missed half of that, I thought you were going to kiss me. All I can see is your lips quivering. I love you. Give me a kiss." Then Jesus leaned in and it was a nice and slow burning kiss making a heat grow inside of my body. He felt so familiar and wonderful.

"I've been waiting for you Jesus to come home all week."

"I missed you too. Now how's Jamie?"

"I feel fine mate. I can't tear her away from you. You've used me Sherie."

"No you haven't. I know Sherie she wouldn't do that," St James said "You've been pestering her for years just to go on a date son."

"I know, but I love her dad as a friend and I wanted her to set me up with a French chippy."

"Look." I said, "We've been eyeing up the women all week together for you. Ooh, la, la, remember?"

"I remember it well. I'll always enjoy our holidays."

"But this is our first one."

"I know but I want others."

"We'll see about that mate," and he lunged in for a very long tongue sarnie to the point of blocking everyone else out.

"I feel like a third wheel mate. I'm going on home."

We broke apart and said, "Fine. We'll see you on Tuesday," and we shared a long kiss again.

"I saw her body mate."

"So what I've seen it loads of times."

"I can't wind you up can I?"

"No. We're in love and I trust her."

"Can you trust me?" asked Jamie.

"I'd trust you with my life mate. Thanks for looking after her."

"So you heard about the holiday?"

"Course I did and she phoned me up to wish me a good night last night."

We then walked to get my luggage and to head towards Thompson's holidays check in for Rome.

"Oh," I said, "I didn't say goodbye to Jamie."

"It's ok." Jesus said.

"No it's not. I'll just tap in 886742 and say goodbye."

"Isn't that Peter's number?" Jesus asked.

"You're right. Oh god what was Jamie's. I think it's something 72468."

"It's 77," said Jamie. "I followed you to say goodbye," and he lunged at me to give me a kiss but I pulled my head away quicker.

"I told you I saw her in the nude."

"What did you just walk in on her?" asked Jesus.

"Well yeah. It wasn't pre-planned."

"I love seeing her naked too mate. Would you like a fight?"

"No I bloody well wouldn't. I'm a wimp you know that."

"Go on then. Have a swing." And his swing went wild and hit me in the face.

"Ow. I like you less."

"I'm sorry Sherie." Jamie said in Urdu.

"It's ok. I'll always have a soft spot for you," and we had a good conversation in Urdu and Jamie's eyes glazed over and said in English. "We'll have another holiday as my family and I are moving to France to live. We all hated that school anyway and dad got fed up of trying to change their rules. He didn't like them and mum would follow dad to the ends of the earth."

"I'll really miss you." I'd said. "You're the bestest friend a girl could have."

He said, "I know. Now can I call you Sher?" and I giggled, "Of course you can." And I walked in to the airport with my arms linked with two of my favourite friends.

Now in the car that turned up with Jesus we travelled to Utopians palace grounds and Jesus quarters to his room. I'd never been in before and got shown around his private living quarters. I said, "Wow! This looks amazing. My quarters aren't as spacious as this. I love you Jesus and not just because of your wealth. It's because I've known you for years and I want an engagement."

"I'd love that. I love you too. Now I've got a bottle of wine."

"No more please."

"I didn't mean right now. I was saving myself just for you."

"So was I till hopefully our wedding night."

"Me too but I need a cuddle and a kiss," so I pulled him to me and rammed my tongue down his throat so hard and so fast I pushed him over right onto his bed and we rolled around.

"I wanna make love to you," as he said coming up for air.

"But?"

"But what?"

"I felt a 'but' coming," I said.

"We want to wait don't we?"

"Well I've been working on a wedding night surprise at perhaps twenty five."

"I want to marry you now. Just to get my eight year down the road surprise."

"But do you love me?"

"I'm so hedonistically and wonderfully in love with you." Then I went really quiet as guilt washed over me as I was supposed to be meeting Peter at the cinema to watch Die Hard 10 tomorrow night. I got tempted to cancel my date as I'd said "I love you" for the very first time at a sweet and innocent fifteen.

Now Jamie was there with us and he got all embarrassed. "I'll leave mate."

"Yeah. Please do. I wanna know if my wealth and prominence in society is all she wants," he said to Jamie,

"I'd love to be a bachelor for a while anyway. You never ask me anything personal about myself."

"But everyone knows everything about you and you're a little show off. On all our dates I've seen so much pride in the things you've got and the lifestyle. It is fast paced and I'd love to be able to keep up."

"I've tested you to the hilt. Now Ahmed is not your tool to use to get me if you know what I mean?"

"Well no. I don't understand. I know we're related by marriage but we're not blood relatives and you've always been my favourite as I've rarely ever had to set up dates with you. It's been you who's normally asked me out."

"I know but I'll be curious from now on about your motives," and then I burst into tears.

"But all I've done is done all my dating through the chaperones and parents. I thought I was doing the right thing. I thought we were getting closer and closer each time."

Jesus said, "I love you. I love you very much."

"Yeah I love you too. But it irritates when someone keeps saying that over and over again."

"I didn't know that."

"Well Jamie does as we've settled for a really good friendship."

"But I am jealous. Now what really happened to you this week?"

"Do you want a blow by blow account?"

"Well yeah."

"Well for starters we went with his mum and dad. We all went up the Eiffel Tower and I was sick everywhere. I mean me and Jamie have a good laugh when we're together and I love the fact he knows Urdu."

"I'm not going to ask," He said, "what you did again and that's why you don't want wine because you've had enough this weekend."

"Well yeah."

"Now let me lead you Sherie to getting to know you better and I want you to know me."

"Look excuse me. I am tired and I would really like to go home now. When are you taking me to Rome?"

"We're not going. I've tried too hard with you. It was nicer when we had dates up at the park. I wanted a normal life not jetting off anywhere."

"Well good. Right now I am permanently jet lagged."

"Well that's fine. Do you love me too?"

"I just said yes. Too many times," said I, "and it will piss me off."

"Then I'm not the man for you am I? Because when I am in love in the future my wife will hear I love you every single day."

"You can't just make it a habit though. Jamie learnt that lesson from me. Now we're really good friends."

"Right then you're tighter than tight and where does Peter fit in to this?"

"Well believe it or not. It feels like the whole relationship thing is easier with him. We go on normal dates like to the cinema to hold hands in the back row and I love him too. You're the one always organising these things."

"Believe it or not I had something special to ask you but it'll have to wait."

"Like what? We're only fifteen and I feel more in love with you every time you spoil me with fantastic dates, but right now I just want to go home. Oh and by the way my best holidays with you are when we go back to Pakistan and I get to show you off to my family then I can puff my chest out too."

"Now I'm off," said Jamie, "I bet you didn't know that I'm off to live in France."

"No I didn't mate."

"Right. I gotta go home. Will someone walk me there?"

"I will mate."

I then went in doors and it felt wonderful to be at home. Then in my room I stripped off quickly and dived in to a freshly cleaned bed and promptly fell asleep.

Two days later I actually started to feel refreshed. It was a Sunday and I wanted to go to church of where Jamie goes. I couldn't remember what it was called but I knew I had to walk through the large Swing Set Park.

"Right." I said to myself, "I better put on something to day that looks amazing." I chose a sky blue dress and same coloured kitten heeled shoes and I wrapped my sash around my neck like a scarf and put on a bit of make-up. I felt beautiful and started out towards Saint Schools' church on the other side of the park. I'd braided my hair all down one side and put on some perfume. Today was the day to say goodbye and I was desperate to get their new address to write letters as I promised to stay in touch. The church had no denomination to it and included different parts of all churches services. I could even get to say my favourite Meccan prayer.

CHAPTER SEVEN

At the service I saw that Jamie, with his parents had turned up first along with his aunties and uncles taking up the front two rows of seats along with his cousins.

I got up and led the prayers this morning by taking up my prayer mat that was on the pews. I faced east and began to say, "Let's all pray to Mecca," and everyone joined in wailing. It was bliss to my ears and was aware of the men ogling my little bum. I got up red cheeked and embarrassed glad I got to take part in the service. Then the peace was taken and I glowed shaking everyone's hands, saying, "Peace be with you." I had my hijab on my face at that moment and I felt all eyes on me, especially Jesus.

Now the vicar named Ashrad said the sermon and he told us about James gospel and his ministries of how he was a guard of whom went through everything in people's homes to vet out any knives or weapons so that Jesus wouldn't get hurt when going to heal others. Now I found this enthralling as he sounded like an old fashioned hero and I fell in love with the sermon.

Then it was our turn to sing, 'Colours of Day, dawn into the mind, the sun has come up, the night is behind. The evening draws on, the sun disappears, but Jesus is living his spirit is near. So light up the fire and let the flame burn open the door let Jesus return take seeds of his spirit, let the fruit grow, tell the people of Jesus, let his love show.'

I sang that really well and certain stuff was wafted about that made me sneeze. I didn't like it very much. Then we sang 'The Lord is my Shepherd' after a gospel reading. Then we said the Lord's Prayer after the communion was taken and I knelt down to take the bread and the wine. I felt a bit of a fraud as I knew about having

needed confirmation classes first. I went to sit down for the last hymn after the Lord's Prayer which was:
> Abba father
> Hallowed be thy name
> Thy kingdom come
> Thy will be done
> On earth as it is in heaven
> Give us this day our daily bread
> And forgive us our sins
> As we forgive those who sin against us
> And lead us not into temptation
> For thine is the kingdom
> The power and the glory
> Amen.

We sang the last hymn. 'What is on your heart?' Then we all filed out back towards the park. Now I wasn't in the right clothes for the swings but I sat on one anyway and talked to Luke.

"Did you like the service Luke?"

"Well yeah. It was different."

"In what way for you?" and he said "That Meccan prayer is hard."

"It pays to have a voice coach."

"Is that how you do it as well?"

"Well yes. I've grown up with it but I love to sing that prayer and I had voice coach lessons for it."

"Wow. Now do you remember your eleventh party?"

"Vaguely but yes. Why?"

"I knew you did want a little kiss. Do you still want one 'cause you're amazing?"

"You can if you want but I must warn you I'm seeing Jesus and he's a black belt in Tae Kwando."

"Oh. Ok then, but weren't you always seeing him? One last kiss. I'm so used to older women taking the lead. I want to with you."

"Really?"

"Yes. I want your kisses," and I gave him a slap round the face for being so pertinent. Then I stormed off and he started after me. "I'm sorry," but I didn't look back as I'd seen Jesus looking over at us.

"Women," I heard, "Who needs them?"

It was Luke sounding exasperated. Then I saw Peter go over and sit with them. "It's Sherie isn't it?"

He'd said "Yes."

"I should have had a date with her on Saturday night to watch a new James Bond film together but she never showed up."

"I know mate, some women are hard work. I need older women again, but I've asked all of them."

"What about that American Ruth mate?" Peter said.

"I've never thought of her. Every time I see her she looks mysteriously at me."

"That Rachel's the same. Aren't they Sherie's friends?" Peter asked.

"I wonder if Sherie's any good at fixing up dates. She seems to be happiest with Jesus."

"She does doesn't she? And I sometimes see her laugh with that Jamie."

"Isn't he moving to France soon?"

"Well yeah. I'll bet that Sherie has something to do with it. She drives us men mad."

"Did you see her ass in there?" said Luke, "She'll turn anybody's heads but she messes us around."

I overheard all of this.

"I did not mess you around Saturday. I couldn't find you Peter so I just gave up and I thought we were watching a Bollywood move."

"No," he said. "I waited patiently to watch the new James Bond movie."

"Well we must have missed each other and I knew someone was ogling my bottom. You deserved that slap Luke."

"Right. We are trying again with that Ruth and Rachel."

"Well don't ask me to set you up and don't bother going on that date networking site. It works outside school rules."

"What do you mean?" Luke asked.

"I know that the last woman you dated was married. Just ask the chaperones to set you up. Kara's a lovely person she'll go on any date you care to book up especially if it's abroad."

"She must love her job," said Jesus. "My girlfriend isn't thick. We're all off to Canada soon to see Aunt Margaret."

"Who is that?" said Peter.

"It's a relation on my mother's side. Only Jesus knows all about my family. Oh and Peter you're better off with Rachel she's the gobby one who'll actually talk to you and sound more grown up and she isn't afraid of wild animals like I am."

"But you're not are you?" asked Jesus. "We're supposed to be vets in the future."

"Yeah. I am but I want to specialise in cute little household pets like dogs, cats, rabbits, hamsters and gerbils etcetera. Not camels."

"I want to help the wild animals as well as the tame ones. You're gonna have to go Sherie and pick up your luggage. We're off to Canada tonight."

"I can't wait but what happened to that speech that I might be after your money?"

"I know you're not. You're so in love with me."

"Of course I am." I'd said and we linked arms as we got off the swings to walk through the Swing Set Park together to go and say goodbye to Jamie at his quarters.

"Aren't you going to Jamie's leaving party?" I asked Peter and Luke.

"I didn't know about it."

"Well you know where he lives just follow us. Have you got any presents? I've got him a nice Sauvignon Blanc."

"I've got a Dinky toy. A collectible car." Said Luke, "All ready for him and I'll make a beeline for Ruth and get myself puddled. I am tired of always acting mature. Every adult says I'm more mature than anyone else in my year and I want to let my hair down."

"What have you got Jesus?"

"Who said that?" said I.

"It is St James. I need to know because my little Jamie is not getting drunk again."

"But I got Sauvignon Blanc back in Paris and I know he likes it?"

"That's ok. Everyone can have a little bit each," said St James. "I was asking Jesus anyway."

"It's a nice evening. I've booked up some camel rides."

"That's nice sir. I haven't got anything that special just a full magicians box. He asked for one ages ago as he loves doing magic. We used to love it when you would produce coins from behind our ears sir."

"I remember that all too well," and he looked at Jesus with a little wink in his eye.

We all then went inside. There was music playing in the background and everyone already had drinks in their hands. I felt great in one of my favourite dresses with Jesus and we fanned out after giving Jamie our presents. I went straight to Ruth and Rachel. "Hi ya you two. Did you enjoy your last holiday to the states?"

"Well yes," Ruth said, "It is wonderful in Wisconsin. We got to visit our families of whom are still wondering when we get our HRHs."

"I'm not sure how that works actually." I'd said finally twigging as to what one of their arguments used to be about. "I remember when we first got here though and Mohammed telling us we were all to be considered as princes and princesses."

"Is that what he said?" Rachel asked.

"I think so. I mean over the years I've just been obsessed with finding my one true love and taking it from there. I have not wondered about peerage titles."

"Neither have I," said Luke overhearing us. "That's why I've only been after real ladies already with titles and they treat me with a lot of respect not like the giggling and arguing girls in our year."

"You're right though." Said Peter. "I remember that because I remember being told us boys would be princes."

"Is Jamie staying till the end of the year to take his exams Mr Lloyd?"

"Call me James, Sherie and yes he is. In answer to all your questions you've been earning peerages since you came here. Sherie you haven't earned your princess of the Jews title correctly though, but I hear you're staying on at the school for another two years?"

"Well yes. They're letting me teach classes after school teaching biology, like the dissecting of frogs 'cause I'm fascinated by their internal organs. Don't worry we don't kill them." I said as others overheard and gave me daggers. "We find the dead ones and it's important to know and experience looking after internal organs." I was hopping on one foot, "I'm sorry sir but you're putting me on the spot and I need the toilet. Oh I knew about the peerages and I'm a proud Muslim girl."

Now Peter overheard and said, "Look, before you go to the toilet I don't know what I did wrong with you. Can I have another date to clear this up?"

"Not a problem, but I'm off to Canada soon. I love to follow my dreams and will say before I leave. What are your dreams?" and I left for the toilet. When I came back everyone stopped talking and Jamie gave a little speech.

"Now before I go I'd love to say thank you to everyone at this school. I actually want to be an ambassador for peace in France. Not one to blow my own trumpet but I'm multi-lingual. I speak Urdu, French and English and have been head hunted at this school to go to a specialist university in France."

"Wow." Rachel said. "I wish I was that brainy. I'm not good enough for him am I? I was going to ask him out."

Everyone started clapping and came up to Jamie one-by-one to wish him luck for the future.

"I now want to crank this music up." And he put the Urdu music up and blared the place for dancing all night. Loads left early for the camel rides and so did I with Jesus after air kissing Jamie on both cheeks just like my mum always did. It was very chic.

"Can I have a dance Sherie?"

"Of course you can Peter. I've always liked you. Where are you going when you leave school?"

"I'm going to an Arts College."

"Oh. You mean Performing Arts?"

"Well yes. My dreams are to be a drama teacher."

"I didn't realise you liked drama and I know you'd think this a rude question but I learnt all this when I first started at this school. What is your lineage?"

"It's not lineage Sher. It's new money. My parents are famous singers. I wanted you to meet them one day. Now I'm feeling sad. I love you and I'm not going to ask you out again you're too intelligent for me."

My little eyes welled up with tears. I had a choice of following my heart and living out my dreams. Something was going to have to give.

"You've got a large heart Sherie, but I want you to ask for my new address."

"I was going to wait for the right time."

"When?" I said.

"When we take our last exam together."

"What exam?"

"Our Urdu language course. That's next Friday. When are you going to leave?"

"Straight afterwards. Right I want you to have my address now. It's twenty-five Louvre Road, Paris, PF54 5UN. I want to talk to you now. I love you more than anything. Would you come with me to France some times. I'll always come back here for holidays."

"I thoroughly enjoyed our last holiday together but you're bad for my health." I took his hand and went to the fridge and got two wine glasses, and said, "Let's go outside on the terrace." I cracked in to my Sauvignon Blanc I'd saved just for us and served the drinks.

"Let's make a private toast. The best friendship ever," And we clinked glasses and slowly this time we sipped steadily our way through the bottle and shared secret little giggles.

"We got the best out of this school didn't we?" Jamie said.

"My sentiments exactly."

"I want the peerage," he said, "I've actually got the certificate already. Do you want to be Mrs Queen of the Jews?"

"I'd love to be but with Jesus." I'd said.

"I know it's true. Are you using him?"

"Well yeah. For love."

"Right. I didn't expect that."

"He's using me for love too."

"I'm going to go happy knowing you're on the end of a line. My number's going to change to +775496111102."

"I've got it." I'd said, "My address book is finally full. I started this when I first started at this school."

Someone looked out the back door. It was my mum. "Sherie, everyone's going. We want Jamie back inside to say goodbye to everyone."

"I think we've finished this anyway Jamie," I said swaying a bit, "I don't think I can handle my drink. Hold my hand Jamie," and he helped me up from the step. We staggered up the steps laughingly singing our heads off and then we bumped into Rachel and Luke snogging behind a tree. Jamie put his thumb up to them and Luke smiled at us for the briefest of moments. Our eyes glazed over.

"I'm going to see what I can do," said Jamie. "I need clearance for France and destinations are me. I need a clear direction from you Sherie."

"What do you mean?"

"I got life experiences all waiting for me. I need to write home to you. I love you. You're the best friend I've got. Now why don't you go to the airport with me? I'm off to Canada too but not with you in ten years' time to go and live. Now where does Aunt Margaret live?"

"Nova Scotia."

"It's ok. It's far out. I'm going to Ottawa to visit my parents in ten years' time."

"Why are you focusing on ten years' time?"

"Because I am marrying my fiancé. You. In ten years' time."

"It's not going to happen." I'd said.

"Why not?" I saw his puppy dog sad eyes.

"I thought we were friends. Please don't ruin this."

"You've got to go." Jamie said, "You're in my future. I need your love."

"Please don't do this," and I broke down in tears, "Don't go. I'll miss you. I'll miss our friendship. You're being too intense and I actually feel sorry for you and myself. I don't want our friendship ruined. I secretly knew though that's why I kept this friendship light. I am so in love with Jesus."

"I've got to go. I'll see you when you get back from Canada."

"I will." I squeezed his hands and we both burst into tears. "Ten years is a long time you'll meet and fall in love with somebody else."

"You're right. Oh, Sherie. My sweet Sherie. I've understood you better than everyone else." I moved to leave him and sent everybody else home, "Now's not the time for goodbyes. Thank you all for coming."

The music I had turned off and we went in to talk in Urdu out on the balcony. "Why didn't you say this before? You're a wonderful friend. I don't want to ruin this friendship."

"Neither do I. Thanks for doing that Sherie."

"Now tell me about your studies. Then we'll hit into what your ideal woman is like. Pistachios please," I said to a passing waiter. "And you can go home too. Leave it please till tomorrow." The staff groaned and left.

"Right. Talk to me Jamie. How am I your ideal woman?"

"Now I'm glad you asked. You're too in control for me. I need a vulnerable woman I want to look after."

I gave him my clean hanky. I thought he was going to break down in tears.

"I think you need someone to take control of you and be more traditional."

"You've hit the nail on the head," Jamie said, "I like traditional housewives."

"Well I'm. I've been dreaming of being a high flyer. Jesus and I are going to be vets eventually in Texas and do a lot of social functions as part of a traditional prince and princess lifestyle. I've had this mapped out all along and Peter I nearly chose until I realised he's too traditional for me too. I am not a little wifey just always barefoot and pregnant."

"Right I'm glad we cleared this little one up. You had me scared for a minute."

"Why?" I asked.

"I thought you're always beautiful and full of life and happiness."

Jesus was in the kitchen overhearing us and saw us embrace.

"Come on." He said, "My private jet is waiting."

"You're right," and I dabbed a tear falling from my left eye with my napkin and sniffed re-adjusting my clothes. "I gotta go." I said to Jamie.

"You're beautiful woman Sherie," and he blubbed everywhere. He tore at my heart.

"Did you hear everything Jesus?" I'd said.

"Let's leave him alone." Jesus said.

"But I don't want to. He's my friend and vulnerable."

"I got to go. Please leave," said Jamie. He'd realised his mistake. Sherie kept things together. He couldn't.

"I love you." Jamie said, "I'm too ardent for you."

I took his hands and stared into his eyes and we held each other's stare. "I never fully knew how much you meant that. I thought that if I kept things light, was always honest and told you about my life even with Jesus. Always being strong you'd get the message that I'm not in love with you."

"Please leave."

I bowed my head in acquiescence and Jesus took my hand as I held up my skirt and we left him alone.

"I feel bloody embarrassed." I heard from him as Jesus and I headed for my quarters to pick up my luggage I never unloaded to go off again. We walked through the Swing Set Park linking arms feeling romantic as Jesus told me we were to take a limousine down to the hangers and I could see a tear in his eyes too.

"I am really proud of you. I wish you hadn't encouraged that relationship."

I turned my head and nuzzled into his arm. "I'm really going to miss that friendship," and I was tempted to scratch out Jamie's new address and number.

"Don't do it," Jesus said, "Hold on to it. I love you. I realise you need that friendship."

"But I didn't realise his depth of feeling for me. I don't really need my little black book any more. I've made my choice. It's you. It always was."

"Don't get rid of it. It'll be a present for my younger sister. You've got a lot of numbers."

"I need to update it. A lot of these numbers are out of date."

"I understand now, but it's important."

"What is?"

"My lineage. do you want my money?"

"I want the whole package. All of you Jesus. I love you. You're so wonderful to me and I'm sorry if I never asked for dates from you enough, but I never had to. you love me don't you Jesus?"

"Well yeah, but I have a stipulation. I need you to be integrated more in to my family and our Jewish beliefs."

"I'll try." I looked deeply into his eyes.

"We're here," said Kara and we boarded the plane. Sat down in our seats Jesus looked at me. "If you don't mind we're sharing with Ruth and Rachel. You are my three suitors."

"You're joking!"

"No. I'm choosing. I've been doing this since the beginning and I have three challenges for each of you."

"Are you going to tell us what they are?"

"Yes. You all know me and you're all friends. I want to test our relationships. Now I've got you under my skin."

"I've got you under my skin," said I. "I love you. Why are you doing this?"

"Well. Have you had a system to choose who you love the most?"

"Well yeah. Kisses. I've rated them out of ten," I said, "Yours is a definite ten out of ten."

"That's brilliant, but what about compatibility and pretending we're poor for a while. Would you get bored with my company?"

I gulped, "I'd let down Peter over this issue. He didn't seem exciting enough for me."

"How much did you rate him with kisses?"

"Well the last time I was with him it was a seven and a half," said Rachel.

"I thought eight out of ten," said Ruth.

"And what about you Sherie?"

I turned my head and blushed, "About a nine." I am hating this I'd said in my head and I held my head in my hands. The other two girls didn't seem worried.

"I love you Jesus." I'd said and realised I was going to go down the road poor Jamie went lost and broken over the one person I'd fallen in love with.

"Now you know how it feels to be used Sherie."

"But you were the one who chased me a lot." The other two were beaming confidently but my heart felt torn. This felt cruel and I wanted to cry but realised my situation being stuck on a private plane feeling like I was in a viper's pit.

"Don't worry," said Ruth to me. "We'll get through this. I'll still be your friend."

"So will I." said Rachel misreading my tears. They obviously thought I was worried our friendship would fall apart.

"You obviously know what's going on."

"He's testing our friendship if he happened to choose one of us for a future wife."

"But I'm totally hating this all ready. I wish I was at home."

"What would you say if I told you I was married all ready?"

"I'd give up and cry myself to sleep," said little Ruth.

"I like the answer," he'd said. "Now Rachel what would you do?"

"I think I'd kill myself."

"Right now Sherie."

I tried to ignore him but simply said, "But you're not married. I've bought every cutting in every paper about you."

"I didn't know that, but it's true."

"You're lying," I spat back at him and everyone was shocked. Little Ruth eyed him up and down.

"It's me isn't it?"

"No," he'd said.

"But you proposed to me once."

I gasped and put my hand to my throat, "This can't be happening," I thought. "This is cruel to me."

Now Jesus looked shocked, "Look. I'm dealing with Ruth."

"Look, if we weren't high above international waters I'd demand to get off this plane now."

"It's not true," he said.

"You obviously said something to her." I said with my voice getting louder. "We were all friends you know."

"I am pissed off," he said, "Some girls have treated me like a joke."

"Is that about Mount Rushmore?"

"No." he'd said.

The other two said, "What about Mount Rushmore? We should know that one."

"He took me there once and he became ill."

"We didn't know that. he always had a hard man routine for us."

"He sometimes comes across as vulnerable to me. yes, sometimes a bit silly, other times self-absorbed."

"Like when?" he'd said.

"Well when you used to puff your little chest out when you were younger obviously glowing about your wealth and showing it off. The first time my heart leapt into my throat, you were so sweet but too self-absorbed to notice my little eyes lighting up at you. Looking like the big man like your dad."

"I've got this covered," he said. "Now I've got to go another way with you haven't I? because you don't shut up."

"I have got a brain cell you know, and I've had plans with you. If you remember for us both to be vets together."

"I forgot that one. But how fanciable am I?"

I blushed and looked out the window.

Ruth spoke up, "You've been amazing in bed," she said. "In my head."

"Me too." Said Rachel.

"Have you thought about it Sherie?"

"Do I have to do this now?"

"Well no, but I'll keep on asking."

"Could I have some wine please? Before I do I'm still inebriated a bit from earlier anyway."

"Fine," he said, "I only found out recently it's Sauvignon Blanc."

After a swig I felt bold enough to ask.

"Have you ever got any real emotion Jesus?"

"What do you mean?"

"Don't you ever get jealous?" and I ground my teeth.

"Well yeah." Now Ruth and Rachel chipped, "He gets jealous all the time around us. He won't let other men near us."

"Fine, you're welcome to him but," and I looked him squarely in the eye, "I have thoroughly upset my bestest friend in the last two hours and at least you could have was shown some jealousy. Whatever he showed to you was just an act," and I aimed my darts at the girls.

"What best friend? We thought we were your best friends."

"Actually it's Jamie the one you two always say is weird, too intense and creepy. I love him to bits." I desperately wanted to break down in tears. "Not now please Jesus, please. I'm already in bits letting him down over you."

"Right. This is back firing a little bit, but I need some love like the love you showed him."

"He's a friend," and I over enunciated every single word, "I had to leave him in bits over us."

"Right. It's true. Right, I wanna go another way now," he looked me hard in the face, "A fart what does that mean to you?"

"Something bloody embarrassing. At least Jamie has a sense of humour and I've always tried to laugh with you."

"It's at me." He said. "I've always said that to you."

"No, it isn't." Then refusing to go down Jamie's route desperate to hold on to me. I let rip into him. "You've always had a cardboard cut-out personality to me anyway. You've never ever asked me what makes me laugh anyway and I can't help it if Jamie's more intelligent than you." I was desperate to get a stronger reaction from him as I'd been upset over Jamie.

"Are you more in love with Jamie than me?"

"Right now yes."

"Right. I've got to go to the toilet."

"Well arrive soon" I said absentmindedly wishing he'd stay in there for the rest of the trip.

"Sherie. Are you alright? We both know you love him." Said Rachel.

"Who? Jamie?"

"Well yeah." They'd said. "Have you made love to him?"

"No. Jamie is my intellectual equal that's what the adults used to say so I always loved to pick his brains. Have a bloody good laugh and say sometimes that I love him too. When I'd get drunk over a bottle of wine."

"Now why always get wine involved?" said Ruth.

"The chaperones wouldn't allow it."

"But his chaperone was his dad and he always didn't mind. He hated that school and was always changing rules for us. I'd convinced him sometimes to change."

"Well what?"

"Like letting the Muslim girls wear their hijabs in normal churches and giving anyone in school to lead a morning's school prayers."

"I didn't know that," said Rachel.

"I even convinced him that I cared about religious indifferences."

"Wow," said Rachel and Jesus together as he came out of the latrines.

"I want to go another way."

Now with Rachel being quick said sarcastically. "Go puff out your chest some other way," she said and me and her just laughed and then to go another way myself I'd said, "What do you think of Peter?" Now Rachel had been knocking back the complimentary champagne.

"Cor, he's amazing at singing and has a wonderful tanned chest." Ruth caught on.

"I thought he was a 10 out of 10."

"Now Sherie. Let's just relax and not take these tests too seriously. That's why we smiled. He hasn't got a bride already has he?" Said Rachel understanding what was going on.

Jesus said, "I am married to the Jewish religion."

"I thought you worried about integration," said Rachel. "I've had political debates with you before."

"Yes that question wasn't aimed at you Rachel."

"How would you like a little harem with me?" and he winked at me.

"I'm not dignifying that question with an answer," and got all snotty.

"Vet or lawyer?" asked Ruth.

"Oh," he said. "I always said vet to Sherie."

"I thought you were ruling the world one day," Said Ruth.

"Right Ruth. I know how to handle you but you get a bit boring sometimes. I love Rachel's spaghetti arms, so a lot of this is aimed at Sherie.

"Well we've always thought that she is a bit uptight."

Rachel piped up. "You've always told me you'd like a ménage a trois. Now Sherie has he ever tried it on with you?"

"He's kissed me once or twice," and I blushed. "Well he is my 10 out of 10."

"Ah I remember," she said.

"Trust me I would never welcome sex talk. It's above me. I was told by Luke that I'm a very sensual woman. So I've let my body speak for me but Jesus never says anything to me or even comes on to me so I use my sensual French kisses that Luke said he liked about me."

"Oh yeah," They both said looking that they were spoiling for a fight. My head was swimming and I was getting braver. I wanted Jesus to suffer for this. Then I started to feel sick.

"I need the bathroom. Excuse me ma'am could you get me some water please?" and I received some still water before heading to the ladies to throw up. My friends started laughing.

When I came out of the toilet I pushed my seat back, had my water and asked for my alka-seltzers. I picked up my black mask and basically told everyone I needed to sleep and I soon drifted off.

When I woke up eight hours later I was dying tell my friends my recent dream or was it true? I needed to ask. Curiosity pushed me.

"I think I was dreaming but did Jesus mention whips, chains, and tit tape?" I felt scared and wanted my mum.

"No." Jesus said, "I was just telling them about harems and a book called Fifty Shades of Grey."

"I'm glad I was asleep."

"Did I shock you girls?"

"Well yeah. It was just after you gave English breakfast tea to us. We've been laughing and wondering about you Jesus."

"Who can see themselves doing that with me?"

Oddly enough my stomach heaved again. "Ugh." I groaned. "Please. I don't want to know," and I visualised a dance I watched on Superman once that Lois Lane tried on Clark Kent.

"Since we're on fantasies," I'd said. "I always fantasise about a winning seduction technique with Jesus."

"What was it?" he asked.

"Not telling you, but if you marry me you'll get it every month." Finally realising that these challenges need to be matched with challenges of my own. "Would you wait till our wedding night to find out?"

"I have found you at last," he said, "I've never seen this feisty side of you. Now first challenge is that a horde of press, nasty ones keep following me around. I need to know how you'd handle them, because I will have to put up with them my whole life."

CHAPTER EIGHT

"I've been wanting to go another way for a long time," said Jesus as we all pulled up to our hotel called Wendy Emily Lloyds which made me think of my Jamie.

"Now," He said. "Did you ever kiss Luke?"

"Can we please do this in the lounge later waiting for our table?"

"Not this time," he said. "You've avoided disaster for a long time."

"What do you mean?" I'd said while picking up my keys for my room. "look I need a shower. A change of clothes and a dry cleaner."

"Right." He'd said. "I'll wait. Right. I've got two more challenges."

"I still don't know what the first one was and I need a bath," said Ruth and all us girls all scarpered up to our adjoining rooms and giggled all up the stairs. I said. "I think I passed all of them anyway."

"What do you mean?"

"Well. If we'd all said we're playing ball or yeah we can pass that easily we might not be in this mess," said Rachel.

"Pardon et moi? As I was gonna say I could have done all of this in French or Urdu."

"What's Urdu?" said Ruth.

"Uuh, Ruth. You know those strange words I taught you years ago at my eleventh party. That's my home language." I picked up the edge of my dress to walk up the stairs to my room. "My Jamie would have helped me to avoid this and Peter certainly wouldn't have been crazy enough to do this." I sighed wishing for the moon at that point. A shower, no more alcohol and a little treat. That's what Jesus promised me would come my way. My head was with Peter right now but my heart was slowly breaking over vindictive Jesus. I could have done with Jamie for a really good laugh. Even Luke seemed like a better option.

When I got in I cried into my pillow not thinking of myself but my Jamie. All I could think of was our friendship was over and I wept very hard into my pillow with feelings of regret. I wished it could have been him I'd fallen in love with then my love life wouldn't have been so complicated. I didn't even feel hungry as I'd just cried myself into sleep.

Two days later I got up without jet lag and tiredness finally gone. I'd had a wonderful shower that lasted for an hour. I tried to muster a little song in my head from modern music. I had this idea for ages as to how to seduce Jesus on our wedding night but wasn't sure if he'd want to marry me anymore. With my mind made up I decided to let him take my virginity before marriage and had to find a way to tell him that I wanted him. I was going against every piece of advice I'd had from adults and wondered how I was going to get pass Kara to see him.

I'd heard doors slamming outside and shouting. "They're here. Downstairs in the lobby now," and it was a bodyguard.

Downstairs in the lobby it looked like the whole world's press turned up. Now there was a long desk that had seven chairs along it and Rachel, Ruth and I had to sit on the left hand side, Kara next to us, Jesus in the middle with our bodyguards standing up behind and two senators on the other two chairs. I wandered what this was going to be about and remembered opening the new vets and park in Texas and knew that I was going to have to do this simply.

Now the press were asking us about Utopia school and wondered about the ethics of the school and I wandered why the founders of the school or Mohammed our head teacher wasn't there. We were waiting for them to turn up but this was impromptu Kara had said. "It should have been this afternoon when Graham Oliver Davidson and Mohammed were expected and Mary and Joseph were here.

"Right. We need to talk with Jesus and his suitors. Sherie. They talk about you a lot at this school why do you think that might be?"

I cleared my throat, "Well I'm a straight A student and multi-lingual and am training to stay on at the school as a teacher for two years in biology. I really want to be a vet and I've played the school system about integration and arranged marriages the adults way. I've always played by the rules."

"So you're sixteen year old virgin? That's a rare thing these days," a dirty old reporter laughed about.

"I take love very seriously," I'd said, "And want no shame on my family. I want to marry at twenty five years old and keep myself chaste till then." I proudly stuck out my chin. I worried about little Ruth who was always shy and Rachel who could run at the mouth but the next ten minutes seemed like hours as the reporters scratched their heads. Then Jesus spoke up. "This interview's over," he said and we all got up and went back to the hotel.

Jesus came up to me and said. "Well done." I sank into him for a cuddle quite automatically and said, "I want to discuss sex with you. It finally hit me in the interview that I'm a prude. That's what they'll say about me won't they? But a love life should be no-one else's business. I know I've never talked about this with you before but I need to. You're my boyfriend."

"Let me speak. It was brave of you to open up about a sensitive subject."

"But I know that second journalist was going to take the piss out of us. It was obvious."

"I know. You're the best representative for the school. We thought that three modern girls with different attitudes could portray the school as hip and modern. I really thought my gobby Rachel would have said something."

"I love you," we both said together.

"To the world I said we've got to wait and I hate lying but sex embarrasses me and I'd like to seduce it's all I've ever tried to do."

"I know. You're lovely. I got torn for a while. You didn't insist on many dates."

"I know but in a way I was going through something similar with Peter and Luke. Jamie was never in the picture but I really believe I've lost his friendship and I'm really sad."

"I was really jealous of him and wanted you jealous of Ruth and Rachel. I've still got to test these relationships but at least now I know what you want. You told the whole world's press you don't want sex."

"I know, just keep cuddling me. I want it but feel there's a lot of pressure on me to be perfect. I've always had to do the right thing and as a middle child I've learnt to be a peace keeper."

"Sex is important to me and we'd have privacy."

"But I've fought against hypocrisy for a long time now. I need to tell you again I've been practicing seduction techniques and I've building this all up to a really famous technique I know you'll love ready for our wedding night."

"What is it?"

"I can't tell you. It's a surprise. If you can't wait for me I can't think of two other nicer girls you could end up with than Ruth and Rachel, but they're really close."

"I know and you've got a really good friendship."

"Just to let you know don't string me along I can't wait forever. I've got other options with someone who's prepared to wait for that something special to happen."

"Now I've got you under my skin. I'd love lovemaking with you."

"I've got to ask, even though I thought I knew you. Are you a virgin?"

"No." he said, "Ruth's very obliging and Rachel is too."

"Don't you see lovemaking as special with the right woman? I thought that was me. I was shocked. After all your pursuing of me you saw my best friends too. I'm really hurt."

"I've seen you naked loads of times."

"Does it encourage fantasies."

"Well yeah. I've got to know why are you talking about this?"

"That interview had got me to thinking that the world doesn't mind openly discussing sex and I want to be an adult about this and not shy away from this issue. But whoever I end up marrying has to see that lovemaking was one special woman is totally worth it and I wanted you to say that I'd be worth waiting for."

"I'm sorry. This is why I'm doing these challenges of doing things together. I need a wife who'll stand by me."

"That's what I want from a husband." I wanted to break down in tears again. "I'd thought this chasing of me was you telling me I was your special girl."

"Well you're not."

"We were going to be vets together. You just said you love me, or don't those words mean anything to you?"

"Of course they do but I've been sleeping around a bit. I like sampling the goods." I just saw red and slapped him round the face and stormed off back to my room. I suddenly realised that nothing is sacred any more. I loved my faith and wanted to dedicate my whole life to doing things properly.

Now downstairs Jesus was shocked and I saw him later knocking back whiskies at the bar.

"I didn't know you like whiskies. I prefer wine."

He said. " I know. Now that Peter and Luke are out of the way will you be mine?"

"No and I liked Jamie's attitude better. At least he's honest with his feelings and was willing to hold out for me. I wish I could have felt that for him."

"Right. I've got to make a choice too. You drive me to distraction Ms Sherie-Marie Kumar. I want to own you and be your first, your last, your everything."

In the back of my mind I wondered what Ruth and Rachel were up to, so I just hung my head and wanted to find them. I put my head up and said to him. "I've heard Peter and Luke on about this. Did you see anything in me at all? You don't mention love and when you said it earlier I thought you meant you just say that to get us into bed?" Feeling angry again I just stormed off and wanted to avoid people. I hit another bar and started knocking back the wine and another little creepy reporter came over.

"I didn't buy that routine," and he touched my legs up. I got so angry and actually punched him in the face.

"That's going in the paper."

"No. It's not. I'll pursue you through the courts for slander. You've no proof I hit you."

"You're right. I won't print it princess but I overheard that Ruth and Rachel are loose."

"Leave them alone."

"No."

I grinned wildly after having two glasses of wine. "Do that and miss out on a better story. Jesus has bought three girlfriends with him that have three challenges to help him work out who he really wants to marry. I know you're only from a tattler and this should make front page news. I'll give you the inside story," and I sat there for ages talking to him.

"You've got to be kidding me?"

"No." and I slithered off my seat.

"Help me. I need to know in advance what these challenges might be." I saw his hand itching to push itself up my back and I swiped his hand away.

"I was only helping you to get up."

"Oh. You're right. My head's spinning. I want my Jamie."

"That sounds intriguing."

"He's my best, best friend but I think I've lost him."

"Now let me carry you up to your room. There's going to be an article about underage drinking at this school."

"Whatever," my head was pounding. "I want to go to bed."

Jesus stormed over and fists started flying. I escaped and ran up to my room. There was a lot of shouting downstairs. I groaned, some disaster was bound to have happened. I've got desires to be a nun.

Back in my room I threw up all over my best clothes we had been told to put on today. It was wine red with a sari over it and I suddenly had a desire for lunch. I had to get in the shower and left my clothes out for laundry service. Then I swilled my mouth out and cleaned my teeth. Then I remembered where my friends went. It was to the pool outside. I got out my bright red bikini with dangly gold bits on them. A little bit of retro. I thought. Then I put an orange and white tie-dyed patterned dress on over the top. Then took an Alka-Seltzer. My mind started to clear. I'd made a disaster of today and hoped Graham Oliver's press team had dealt with him.

My phone rang. It was mum.

"How are you doing love?"

"Wonderful mum. It's nice to hear from you. How are you doing?"

"We're here in Canada with your Aunty Margaret."

"We're coming over in three days' time."

"We'll make sure we're in."

"I love that mum."

"Been enjoying yourself?"

"Well yes. Every minute. We had an impromptu press call this morning. I think Mohammed and Graham Oliver are taking the second one. A mess has to be cleared up."

"What sort of mess love?"

"Oh Jesus and a reporter got into a fight."

"Over you?"

"Well yes, actually. He was being a bit creepy."

"You sound a bit unwell love."

"I'm ok mum, that fight shook me up a bit. I mean just before I had to slap him round the face."

"You're joking?"

"No mum and Jesus has got me in a pickle this weekend. I'd been looking forward to a bit of romance but Ruth and Rachel are here and apparently Jesus quite calmly said that he'd slept with both of them. I am really upset."

"Maybe he's not the one for you then. You could always cut your trip short and join us in Nova Scotia."

"God I'd love that mum. I need to ring Jamie. I'm really frightened I've lost his friendship."

"Come on over with us."

"I'd love to mum. I'll see if I can sort something else out."

I got out my iPad and got into the flight's page. I found one flight in two hours' time but I thought I'd need someone with me and everyone else had plans already. I dialled the number for Kara's mobile.

"Karla. I need a favour?"

"Anything for you."

"Have the press gone yet?"

"Well yes."

"I need hiking clothes. Where can I get them?"

"Well in town."

"I need Ruth, and Rachel to go into town with me."

"Why?"

"I've figured out my next challenge, I wish they'd warned me. Are my friends by the pool?"

"Well yes. What challenges? The founder of the school is on about them downstairs."

"I thought this would happen. I've had a fracas with a reporter and me and my friends have to prepare ourselves." I put on my expensive Pagan perfume and put my hoop earrings on. I got my hijab. I realised that to get outside I was going to need it. I walked quite fast and purposefully outside and spotted my friends coming towards me and I got a surprise when I saw Jesus. He had a black eye. My heart went out to him. "What happened?"

"Dad's suing that reporter."

"I was hoping that would happen."

"But he's been gobbing off about three challenges. What the hell have you said to him? They're still on you know."

"Yes. I've figured that much out. Have you got hiking boots?" and I studied his face for a reaction. "Well yes."

"I've got you. Me and the girls are going to get some."

"Who's organised this?"

"Me and my friends work together. We promised each other we wouldn't fall out over this."

"Why did you tell that reporter about the challenges?"

"I thought it would make you grow up. You are playing with three girls emotions."

"Right. I am getting this. You want to ruin me."

"Yes and The National Enquirer I promised them the exclusive on who's getting your hand in marriage."

"What have I got to do to win this?"

"Sleep with me."

"No. I do things my own way. Mums says I'm turning into a stronger woman because of it. Besides you've still got to let down at least two girls who've slept with you so what was the point?"

"Now Sherie. I am talking to you. I love you."

"Did you say that to the other two?"

"Well yeah."

"Don't say that to me unless you mean it!" I swept passed him and I saw a look of appreciation in his eyes as I met my friends.

"What do you think the next challenge is?" said Rachel. "Well he said that we've got to live like paupers so we're put against the wilds of Nava Scotia."

"That's clever." Rachel said. "Are you coming round the pool with us later?"

"Well yes."

"You look hot." Jesus said "I'm coming with you. I need boots and other things too. Now I've got my own agendas."

"Is that little man still here?"

"No." Jesus said, "I've got a better reporter to follow us. You got a good point Sherie and my black eye was nothing. I made mincemeat out the other guy."

"What paper are they from?"

"A famous magazine of whom will go on in years to come to print everything about the wedding day."

"That's lovely."

"It was organised anyway."

"Yeah well. I got a bit drunk and need some lunch while we're out."

"Do you want to go to a Harvester?"

"Don't they do huge meals?"

"Yes."

"I don't know if I could stomach that, but my tummy's growling for my samosas."

"Oh yeah. The samosas. I love 'em. Right. Are we nearly there Kara?"

"Well yes. Warm coats are going to be needed too."

I had my family's platinum card and all of us had theirs too.

Jesus said, "Why are you buying thick coats?"

"Well it's cold in Nova Scotia it's up near Greenland and near to where Kara originally comes from." Said I.

"Why does she live in Arabia then?" asked Jesus sounding simple.

"It's the best job I've ever had and I don't miss the cold at all." Kara put bluntly. "Plus I have little family left. My mother and a brother who lives in New York."

"Don't you have friends there?"

"Well yes. Once upon a time but we all moved to sunnier climes. We've got everything now?"

"I just need a camera," said Rachel. Now I chipped in. "I've gotten this wrong before as Jesus hires a professional photographer for special memories."

"I didn't know that."

"Where has James taken you with Jamie before? I heard that you went with him once." I said.

"Well that was pretty random," said Rachel "Right. he took me to France once. Why?"

"I was just wondering. I really miss him. I was also going to ask both of you where Jesus has taken you before?"

Ruth said, "Well he has taken me all over the world."

"Me too," said Rachel. "Cor this load is heavy."

"Well do what I do." Said I.

"What give it to the bodyguard?" asked Ruth.

"Well yes. I'm not stupid."

"Right. I have to carry it anyway. There's no-one free to carry for me."

"Look around you," I'd said. "There are three bodyguards for a reason. Do you notice nothing?"

"Well yes," said Ruth.

"Now we're off to Nova Scotia?"

"Well yeah," said Rachel. "We have an itinerary list."

"I never got one."

"We know you are intelligent. You work things out on your own."

All of us friends and Jesus went aboard a light plane with a private pilot.

"Wow," said Rachel, "You can see all around you in this plane."

"I know. It's brilliant." Said Ruth.

"Let's have a look?" I'd said getting on last. It was amazing as the plane took off low in the sky and the pilot told us all about where we were flying over. My friends, Jesus and I oohed and aahed the entire flight until we got to White Tip in Nova Scotia.

When we landed and got off we'd changed into our warmer clothes ready for hiking.

We trudged through snow and loads of fir trees till we got to a massive log house shrouded by a large forest. At the door we kicked our shoes off.

"It is the final challenge looking out for each other." Kara said. "You were right Sherie-Marie. You're a clever girl."

"Well I am getting a master's degree you know," and I laughed thinking of Jesus.

"When are we going to get that?"

"In three years' time. I'll be pushing twenty and I'll learn at university how to let my hair down. you make friends forever there," and I wiggled my bum and winked at Ruth and Rachel feeling clever.

"Why are you being weird?" said Ruth.

"I thought I'd try a new sense of humour on you." I blushed and felt stupid but I was happy. "Ta da! Got you." And I put a hand up for a high five.

"Are you on something?" said Rachel. Lost for words.

"Look I just want a laugh my seduction techniques never work and no-one will get my new sense of humour will they?"

"But you've never had a sense of humour." Kara looked shocked.

"It's a survival three days and before I left mum said try and develop a sense of humour you'll have more fun while you're away and I twigged mountain climbing will be no fun unless I have a laugh."

"It's not mountain climbing."

"I know, but mum guessed we might." I giggled like mad.

"What are you laughing at?" Jesus said.

I said, "Well look at our shit hot bodyguards. They're laughing with me and winking. I'd guessed the challenge and thanks to my shopping trip with you guys we'll all be fine." Wanting to stick my Vs up to Jesus I felt wicked. "No-one's splitting our friendship up so I denounce Jesus." I'd had a bad time emotionally all holiday thinking I'd lost my friendship with Jamie and the truth about Jesus getting physically close with my friends was tearing me apart. I'd really fallen head over heels for Jesus.

Then we went for an evening trek against two miles of snow to the local shop and we bought tea.

"Aah," I'd said, "I don't like sausages and burgers." I said when I got there as they'd picked up packs. "I'm a vegetarian."

"We didn't forget," said Kara. "Soya burgers please."

"Thank you Kara." I'd thought very sweetly of how she liked me because we'd grown close.

"Further into the forest then yeah for a camp fire?" said Ruth.

"Yes," I'd said, "It's got to be hasn't it?" and I got a compass out of my haversack.

"Not today." Kara said, "You've pre-empted enough. Now it'll be two miles before we set up camp."

"I didn't bring any bedding," said Rachel, "And I sleep in the nude."

"Whoa." Said a bodyguard.

"Right that's enough. I have a silky negligée for a nightie. It feels nice against my satin sheets."

"Whey!" said Jesus, "You've never told me that."

"Well I still have ballet lessons." I said making my eyebrows raise up while looking at Jesus. he had a so what look on his face.

"I'm very bendy." I deliberately enunciated. The bodyguards burst out laughing.

"We've been watching your seduction techniques since you were eleven. I think you're actually going to twig one day why they don't work."

I saw Jesus wanted to laugh with them with his glistening blue eyes that felt electric. He'd set my pulse racing. Was he ever going to make love to me?

"Your eyes look like pools glistening in the sun."

"What?" he said.

"Nothing." I'd said blinking.

"Right. Let's sit round the camp fire and sing Inuit songs."

"I'd love to," I said in my head as I sat down on sack cloth with the others. We all had to find sturdy branches before we got there and we put our burgers on the end of them first and held them over the fire. I'd done it very carefully and the others soon felt there mistakes at getting twigs too short. I was getting to feel smug and smiled at Jesus face animated by the fire on the other side of it.

"I love you." I mouthed at him.

CHAPTER NINE

In the morning I got out of bed, survival day was ahead of us. I showered quickly knowing I'd be sinking into a bath later on. I had to be dressed and ready for eight o'clock. Dead on the dot I got downstairs to the lobby and met with the others. I'd put my hair back into a ponytail and a guide said, "Now we're getting in a helicopter."

I felt nervous. "Now have we got everything?" I'd said, "Like a map and a compass."

"Well yes you're all going to have one. Now Rachel you'll get dropped off first, then Ruth with Kara, and Sherie last after Jesus and you've all got to get at the meeting point by eleven o'clock." A shiver went up my spine. This felt like a real challenge for once.

"Now a journalist and a photographer will be following you around so don't hit anyone for looking at you or for thinking they're going to touch you up. You Sherie. I'm looking at you," said the survivalist guide. "We'll convene at eleven o'clock."

Right after Rachel got dropped by a small copse of trees. Ruth and Kara got dropped by an iced over lake. Jesus got put down by a rundown old shack in the middle of nowhere. I was getting scared I had to embrace this challenge but ended up confused when I got dropped by our hotel. I looked at my map and compass in my sack and noticed a CB radio. I tried tuning it in to a frequency. At number two I heard a voice that said. "Are you ready?"

"Yes." I'd said. "I'm West One." I deduced the clue on my radio that I was in the west of Nova Scotia at White Tip. I looked on my map for the 'x' and decided to go in the direction of east and walked quite briskly while always fixating on a point in the distance that the compass said that was to the east. I soon got to a small drift I'd thought it was a hill. I tested it by dragging a big fallen branch towards it and poked it through the snow. It nearly disappeared.

"Right." I thought. "I'd better radio in to say I had completed the first set of directions of which I did. "Over and out." I'd said afterward, then looked at the map again and turned round slowly to the left to find north again. I deduced from the map that the trees in front I had to get through but there was a danger sign I could spy through the trees. I had to try and walk to the warning. Thankfully it was in English and it said avoid the pond. Looking at the compass I realised I'd gone to the west slightly and moved slowly to the right. The north was pointing to the left of me. I frowned and had a really good look around. Squinting into the distance I saw a clearing and there seemed to be a hut which was on the map so without looking down at my map or compass I picked my way back through the trees slowly until I spotted a stag. I felt in my pocket for my silent flash free camera and held my finger down for fifteen shots. I thought I'd better radio in that I'd seen a hut.

"You're going in the right direction," the man said on the end of the line. I desperately wanted to know how the others were doing and stayed still for twenty minutes hearing the others converse on the same frequency. I overheard Kara say they spotted a wooden shack to the west. I laughed with relief. Turned the sound down as I overheard over and out from east one. I walked from where I was quite quickly thinking I'd found the right meeting place. I got there and opened the door. I got a shock. "Jesus what are you doing here?"

"I didn't have to do this challenge. The challenges were for you three girls. You've won. Now sit with me with a piece of fishing wire. We have to catch our lunch."

It wasn't long till Ruth and Kara turned up and Kara had to take over to teach us how to fish. It was easier with her help and we could only fish through the little hole in the cabin floor two at a time.

An hour later Rachel still hadn't shown up and then we heard a helicopter overhead. Kara decided to radio through on her CB radio to find out what was going on. We were already beginning to panic for her.

"A rescue helicopter is out there for her."

"Has she been found yet?"

"No." The man said on the radio, "Now stay where you are and will bring her to you so that we can carry on with the schedule."

"Everything's been put back for over an hour." Kara said to us.

"Can we not go out and search for her?" asked Jesus.

"No." said Kara. "We don't want you all to go missing."

"It's ok." Kara's radio crackled, "We've spotted her in the forest going towards our hotel. We need to pick her up and bring her back to the shack. We all grinned up at her.

"Your turn." I said.

"Pardon?"

"We've all caught our lunch. You have to catch something."

She sat down with Jesus and the rest of us went outside. Kara talked to the helicopter pilot.

"I know that one," I'd said to my friends, "He took me to Mount Rushmore and we're all having photos taken with our fish in a minute aren't we?"

"Yes." Kara said. "But I'm talking a minute."

It wasn't long before Jesus and Rachel let out a shriek of laughter. I had to find out what they were laughing at. They come out and Rachel said, "I caught a big swordfish."

"Wow," we said, "That's all we caught."

"Now can we please?" I said to Kara. "Go back to have lunch now."

"We're not going back to the hotel we're spending one night in an igloo and we're making a fire about a mile away outside this igloo."

When we got there a fire was already crackling away and we sat down. "Who wants to learn how to gut a fish?" a man asked by the fire.

"We all would," except Ruth who looked a bit queasy. He took one of the fish and put it on a slab. He then proceeded to chop his head off then it was sliced under the belly and the bones got pulled out.

Rachel shouted. "I can do that." So the man gave her his knife. She slammed it down rather too hard and the head flew off and a crack appeared on the ice slab. Everybody laughed. The man gave the knife to Ruth who didn't have the strength to cut the head off and when she did with help from the man the insides were full of tripe she was told to clean out. She puked everywhere. It was Jesus's turn. "I was told that I didn't have to do this. These are my challenges for you."

But the Inuit, Kara's brother, called Shanuke just laughed, "You have to prove to your women you can do this," and winked at me. Little Sherie. Inwardly the smell made me feel a bit sick and I watched enthralled. I stared at his strong artistic fingers for what felt ages wondering what it would be like having those hands hold me. I felt sad for Jamie as the emotions tore through me. Inwardly I prayed for him and it was weird that I wasn't surprised that Jesus had, had relations with my two best friends. I wanted relations with him too. I really believed that we'd end up together. I was in a contemplative mood all evening and I seemed frozen inside somehow making me feel connected to the freezing cold weather outside.

That evening in the igloo I got out a note pad and pen to write to Jamie.

Dear Jamie,

I never really believed you were in love with me every time you said it while we were friends. I don't understand why I needed alcohol for our friendship to gel.

I hope you find that special someone in France. I realised that staying in touch could be the worst thing for you at the moment as I believe your feelings are very raw for me.

I still maintain we had a brilliant friendship and I'd like to be remembered, in the long run, that way.

I'll always love you as a friend.
Sherie-Marie XX

I cried for him that evening and realised that I was going to have to change to get Jesus actually interested in me as a woman. I was seventeen years old. I'd watched Rachel with skimpy clothes on over the years and her putting on a trowel worth of make-up all the time. I didn't want to be that brash but she obviously knew how to get what she wanted. Rachel was going back to America if she couldn't find her one true love and go to university to be a lawyer. Ruth was more demure in her lady's outfits and subtle make-up. I noticed her that evening too huddling more to the fire than the rest of us and felt a stab of jealousy as Jesus put his arm around her. She looked so cold as her face turned blue. Was I really more clued up about being an independent woman. I didn't want to choose a man over a career. I wanted both and being bossy and domineering towards men and a complete snob seemed to be me. I'd been the one who was really clued up about these trips and Jesus had taken me on a lot of them. Us girls were sleeping on our own together. The men together too.

In the morning I asked Kara if there was a shop anywhere.

"Wait till we get back."

"But I want to send a letter and a postcard to my parents."

"You'll have to wait unless you want to do this on a computer 'cause we've got one back at the hotel."

"But my parents like to collect the stamps wherever I go."

"I didn't know that." Said Kara, "The plane is actually leaving this evening though. Wait until you get back."

"But I want to send it. My parents like the stamps with the marks on from being posted."

"There's a shop at the hotel. Ask if they can help you."

"Is it downstairs in the lobby?"

"Well yes." I walked downstairs and managed to get eleven pound fifty worth of stamps with different landmarks on. There was one with an Inuit on, a snow hole, the hotel, a polar bear and an igloo for my two lots of mail.

Now on the way home I made a point of sitting next to Jesus and trying to hold his hand. He moved it so that I connected with his thigh and I felt him tense up. I left my hand there anyway. It got all tingly and I had to move it when they served my favourite wine. I wanted to prove to my friends that perhaps something other than friendship went on between Jesus and I. I hit in to the wine of which I shared with my friends and told them that Jesus saw me naked a lot and so did Jamie. It was my seduction techniques.

"How's he doing anyway?" Ruth asked.

"Well last time I heard he was doing really well and had got back into music holding concerts all around France."

We were soon landing back in Arabia. In my quarters I went routing through my bags looking for my feminax pills for my bad stomach cramps. I was upset. Jesus never chose all holiday who he wanted to end with. He wanted to play the field a bit more. I was dejected. I really believed that I'd be front page news in the press of being his fiancé.

"I just couldn't choose," he'd said. My days of being chaperoned with Jesus was over. I'd had my full of men and soon got into my teaching work at my old school while taking my three A-Levels in biology, English and maths.

That morning I set up a lesson looking into a woman's anatomy as part of the curriculum for twelve year olds. I began my lesson by giving out pictures of the insides of a woman and I taught the Latin names of different parts of the body. I even done a quiz at the end of the lesson. I even got out a biology word search just for fun as I marked the papers.

These children were very bright and eight out of ten was the lowest points I had to give. I got them to give themselves a clap before they left class. I had a lesson in the afternoon too. It was arranged for me to do my A-Levels Wednesdays, Thursdays and Fridays while I took lessons on Mondays and Tuesdays and that week I had four classes with four different age ranges. I dealt with horses, sheep, pigs and hamsters for little ones to learn their anatomy. I had fun with the younger ones but I was determined to educate them with the right Latin terms and the other teachers commended me once I told them what I was doing with them. They really liked my teaching techniques. The classes were full of twenty four little ones keen to learn. I came across a little girl of whom was called Marie who was fifteen. She seemed very intense and sharp minded so I thought I'd talk to her parents about the summer school I wanted to run for remedial groups to help them catch up with the rest of their class.

This Marie though seemed autistic but no-one told me if she was. I just kept noticing her OCD behaviour. Her desk had to be perfectly tidy with everything on perpendicular angles. Everything about her seemed perfect but she never wrote anything and my quizzes came back as ten out of ten. The way I ran my lessons I had them copy the words of the whiteboard. Then parrot them back all together then to place them on the internal organs pictures. Her answers were always a, b, or c. It was driving me nuts. She was just not learning the Latin words but I could mark her answers down as being right. The only time she did anything properly was when she'd do her word search while I marked papers.

I had a little team going pushing each other on to better themselves with the quizzes and the word searches. This was my sixteen year olds.

That evening I had a phone call out of the blue. It was Jamie and he sounded really happy. "Sherie guess what. I'm engaged and I'm really happy. I want to pick up with our friendship again. I realise now where I went wrong with you as you'd never said you wanted a physical relationship."

"Well I never and things seemed to have cooled between Jesus and I."

"Did you really love him?"

"I'm not sure I did. I fell in love more with our trips out together. I feel I need to get to know him all over again."

"Come to France with us. I want you to meet her she's my Cherie. She's in the orchestra I play in of whom plays a violin. She's a good laugh and a bloody good kisser. I actually get loads of emulations from her."

"That's brilliant. Congratulations." I felt in a tiz, "So you're in a good place with me now?"

"Well yes. I was going to say invite Jesus and hound him for dates."

"I'll try." I said. "But he doesn't ask me out anymore. He's gone to college in Arabia somewhere and I got to keep my ear to the grape vine to know what he's up to these days. A part of me thinks we'll end up together though."

"When can you leave?"

"I don't really get a holiday. I run school during summer holidays too."

"What about Spring break?"

"I'll try and organise something but I'd feel like a third wheel."

"But I've got a friend called Mark over here who's looking for dates."

"You mean a double date?"

"Well yeah."

"I need to get used to doing certain things myself these days though but I still feel the need for a chaperone, but Kara's busy these days with the schools youngsters.

Sometimes, these days, we go out together on our own for chats."

"Try the last week in October."

"I will. It'll be lovely to see you again. I thought you were in university to be a foreign diplomat? How did you get involved with an orchestra?"

"It's part-time. A bit of a hobby I took up with my girlfriend. I play the grand piano. I'm the centre of attention with her."

"I'll do it. I just need to get into school on a computer during my free time."

"Don't you have a computer?"

"Well no. I do everything I need to do at school."

"When are you going to get there?"

"Tomorrow. I have two classes. I'll book up my flights on my break."

"I'd love to see you. I haven't seen you for nearly a year. I could have done without that letter. I realised in the end that anyway."

"Would you even have time for me?"

"The orchestra's part-time for local concerts, of course I would."

"I've got to let you know that Peter is back on the scene and I'm paying him more attention this time and telling him what I want him to do. It makes sense as I thought once his idea of dates had gotten boring."

"I've got to hang up but I'll get in plenty of Sauvignon Blancs."

I giggled. "That would be nice. How's your parents?"

"They're fine thanks. Anyway, speak to you soon."

"I'm missing you. It's all about work with me at the moment."

"Yes. How's that going?"

"Brilliant. I love it. I'll see you in a few months' time. I'll ring again tonight to confirm my flight schedule so you can come to the airport and meet me." I then put the phone down. I noticed that it was getting late, so I finished sorting out lessons for the next day and took myself off to bed. I thought of trying something different in my lessons tomorrow with simple little crosswords with pictures. I'd downloaded the internal organs of a cow and copied and pasted each organ by numbers to put into a crossword. I also did clues all about surgical techniques for certain ailments with a cow. I'd thought that perhaps this would definitely take an hour but leave me marking time at the end of each lesson.

I went to bed happy that night and thoroughly exhausted. I'd set my alarm for quarter past six as my parents had done from a baby. It was lovely to laze in the bath for an hour before getting up for work.

I walked through the large Swing Set Park that morning to get to the school. I wondered every morning how the other small children ever got to school on time as I watched them on the swing sets. I'd never felt so alive and I started singing Urdu songs as I pushed on to school. I felt happy and my briefcase felt heavy that morning but I wanted posters put up on the walls.

My idea for the crosswords turned out to be a good idea and that afternoon I took out my notes for my biology, English and maths A-Levels. They did advise me to do chemistry as well but I'd booked into university to do chemistry and biology together. I had a plan still to be a vet and I ended up in all Jesus's classrooms. He seemed to act like an immature idiot around me. He never used to be that way when he used to court me, but it seemed the chaperones only bothered with the younger school children.

I confronted Jesus after class one day. "Why do you never ask for dates anymore?"

"I'm waiting for you to take more of an interest in me and I'm going out with other girls now."

"Like who?" I said while choking back tears that were welling up inside of me. "I thought you loved me. Didn't you ever seem to care when you were bedding my friends Ruth and Rachel?"

"No. I'd done all the chasing." I blinked back tears and run off towards home. I'd been saving myself all this time just for him. Everywhere I went, especially the park, there was always couples and I was all on my own. I'd been beginning to like Peter's company more and more. I booked up a fancy restaurant one night for my eighteenth birthday for Peter and I on August 21st. I got dressed up in a silky bright orange dress with an orange sash. I painted my face up and had taken to start getting myself waxed all over, even getting a Brazilian, in case sex ever really did happen with Peter. He was a few months older than me and he was prompt for his date with me turning up at my door dead on quarter to eight. We'd had a candle on the table that evening and I never realised before that he was an only child. I discovered that he wanted a wife and children in his future. We were really bonding well together and I let him walk me home in the moonlight through the Swing Set Park that was lit up in the evenings. It was so romantic and I let him put his arm around me. When he came to my door that night I felt my heart racing expecting that night to be tonight. Mum and dad and my sisters were out all night. I leaned in for a kiss.

"Aah. You smell lovely." Peter said. The kiss was perfunctory but I asked him did he want to come in for coffee and I grinned at him.

"I'd love one." He'd said and with wandering hands he slipped my sari off as we walked indoors. I went straight to my stereo and asked, "What music do you like Peter?" I'd built up a small collection of contemporary music. This couldn't go wrong I'd thought in my head and went to go to the kitchen to pull out an ice bucket with a bottle of Cava in.

"I love contemporary music."

"I've got a favourite of romance music." I thought in my head and put on my headmasters old band he'd played in as a teenager. It was called Mohammed and the wailers. It was dead romantic music and I put it on in the background. I sashayed into the living room with the ice bucket in one hand and two champagne glasses in the other. Intent on having a romantic conversation. We mainly talked about our favourite bands, musicals and operas. He seemed really sweet and as we drank and chatted together nicely he began running his hand up my thigh and it tingled. My head began to swim. It seemed that we were chatting nicely all night. I casually put my arms round his neck and sat on his lap. I giggled.

"Don't laugh at me," he said.

"But I'm enjoying this," so I changed tack and started to dance in the middle of the living room.

"It looks like you've had too much to drink Sherie."

I giggled again. I felt like a naughty school girl and I started to strip. Now I'd had oysters for tea after reading about their aphrodisiac properties but they were repeating on me. I got embarrassed. Peter just jutted out his pelvis and I saw his mighty erection and I just couldn't stop grinning. His knees came apart and I started to slide in between his legs. As soon as I felt a connection I'd felt a warmth and a lot of moisture between his legs. he was still sipping his champagne and I felt like bursting into tears, clearly champagne made me weepy and I didn't want him to see me cry, but he felt huge like a horse and I got scared. This was going to hurt. I could see it coming so I said to him.

"This isn't going to work," and I ran upstairs to the bathroom to be sick. Peter called up from below.

"Are you alright?"

"No. I feel really sick. Please just go home. I love you Peter but I've ruined this haven't I?"

It took me ages to clean up and swill my mouth round, clean my teeth and slip into clean silky pyjamas. I went downstairs crying my eyes out. "I've ruined this haven't I? But I'm still a virgin and I wanted this to be so special." I poured my heart out to him. "Look," I'd said, "I've been in love with Jesus forever. I thought that I was getting over him. This isn't going to work. I think I love you too Peter but I feel like I have to try so hard though just to lose my virginity and it doesn't feel right with you at the moment 'cause I can't get Jesus out of my head. I'm sorry."

"I'm sorry too. I'm going. I won't be used."

"It's never going to happen is it?" As he left I slumped to the floor by the front door and burst into floods of tears. It was over. I crawled up to bed. I slept soundly that night on my own crying myself to sleep. I hated Jesus for making me believe for years that he really wanted me.

"Dear God," I prayed. "Please will I ever get a one, one true love in Jesus. I love him so much. He's in my mind and my heart all the time. I love him so much. Why are all my relationships with the opposite sex so hard," and I found myself saying the Lord's Prayer for once. I'd made a pact with myself to learn about the Jewish religion even though Jesus made no bones about his faith at all with me.

CHAPTER TEN

The school year flew by. I'd been to France with Jamie and there'd been no spark like there used to be. His girlfriend Cherie was really stuck up and chic. I wanted to staple things to her head but ended up matching her snobbishness, and I wound up really liking her. At one point in the conversation the boys got bored with us and congregated in the kitchen over lager as Jamie was setting me up with a man called Mark. We switched between talking in French and English and I learned all about her life. She was fascinating as Cherie had travelled all over the world to me and she taught me what I asked for all about her French life. She'd grown up living in a chateau and in her cellar were wines. Her dad was a connoisseur and she introduced me to a nice and fruity claret. We soon hit the bottle and had a laugh. Jamie came in with Mark. My left eyebrow went up and I smiled at Mark.

"What do you do for a living?"

"I work in the Stock Markets."

"Mark's worth a fortune," Jamie said and he kissed Cherie and tongued her. Mark and I got jealous and I said to him as a dare. "Why don't we kiss?"

He'd said "I'd love to." I looked around me wondering if Karen and James had come back like the good old days as chaperones.

Mark's eyebrows went up and he grinned wildly. I took a gulp of Dutch courage and he gently placed his arm around my waist. I giddily leaned into him.

"We're going to bed," Jamie said looking pleased with himself.

Mark's body felt hot and he rammed his tongue down my throat. I started to choke. "Oh I'm sorry was that too big for you?"

My cheeks were burning and he had to give me the Heimlich manoeuvre. As I calmed down with a glass of water Mark said, "We'll keep clear heads shall we?"

Turned out his surname was Kasabad and he was from India. We had a brilliant Urdu and English conversation. Turned out that he had five sisters and an older brother. I told him that I had two sisters and an older brother too. he had a really deep throated laugh and my insides melted. He sounded really upper class. I told him that I was in university studying to be a vet. I told him all about my life. The huge Swing Set Park and the school that I went to. he seemed very amused when I told him all about my dates with the school chaperones and how restrictive it made me feel around the opposite sex. He laughed when I told him all about my seduction techniques. I thought, "Shit not another friend," and I tried again for a kiss.

"Put your glass down." I'd said.

"Pardon et moi?" he said and he grinned at me. "Voulez-vous couche avec moi ce'st soir?"

My eyes glazed over, "I'd love to." I said as we continued to flirt.

"I absolutely adore you," he said. "Jamie told me you were interested in fine art. Can I take you to the Louvre tomorrow?"

"I'd love to." I beamed up to him. By the time we finished talking about art it was five o'clock in the morning.

"I'm shattered. Can we go out this afternoon instead?"

"I'd love to. Come to bed with me, now." I sobered up a bit and said, "Wow, at least we could have that shower together later."

"I'm planning on it," and I headily followed him to his room. He pulled back the top corner of the duvet. "Do all you boys live in hotels or something?" Then it hit me as I asked, "Have you had many lovers?"

"I have and I know what to do with them."

"Look before you start will you marry me?"

"Yes," he said, "Will you marry me?"

"I'd love to. Let's find a Town Hall tomorrow."

"What for?"

"Marriage. I cannot lose my virginity until I get married."

"No." he said.

"I don't understand. I could really love you and my parents would approve."

"Give it a year and we'll have a big white wedding."

"Ah the man of my dreams. Mark and Sherie that's what they'll call us." Then I passed out on the bed with my silk dress on that was orange. I felt Mark undressing me as he then pulled the covers over. He then got on his phone.

"Look mate. You didn't tell me that she's an innocent."

"Did I not say anything?"

"Well no."

"Look she goes home in two days right?"

"Well yeah."

"I've only just met her and she's talking about weddings already. She seems really sweet. I can't seduce her like all my other conquests. Why didn't you tell me?"

"I thought she'd lost it to Jesus. He said he'd seen her body thousands of times."

"He could have meant it in his head after seeing her naked the once. I've left her in a satin negligée. God she looks beautiful. How many boyfriends did you say she had?"

"It's three, Jesus, Peter and Luke."

"Never you?"

"I'd tried mate as a friend to be something more."

"She's asleep now and dreaming of Jesus. Sherie's saying rescue me Jesus. Is there a real man called Jesus Henry William?"

"Well yes. We used to go to school together."

"Did she ever talk about weddings a lot?"

"Not with me mate. She nearly turned me into an alcoholic. I had to find someone else and I love my Cherie who's working to be a translator in parliament over here with me."

"I've got to ask. Will she remember we'd said we'd get married in the morning?"

"She's bloody intelligent mate she knows what she's doing."

"Then she must really want an engagement. Would an engagement ring get her into bed?"

"I don't know. You might be down the aisle before you get it mate."

"She's a nice girl and everything. We really connected. Is this Jesus a hard man 'cause I might have to fight him off. I'll talk again in the morning. Does drink normally go straight to her head?"

"Well yeah, she gets all nice and soft and flirty. She's ripped my heart out but it made me wake up and find a soul mate in my Cherie. We're happily engaged."

"When's the wedding?"

"In May next year mate. Do you really want to get married?"

"My mum and dad would approve. Deep down they always wanted me to marry a Muslim girl."

"You're going to have a fight on your hands mate."

"Why? With whom?"

"Me. I still love her, please don't mess her about."

"But I could get an Arabian passport out of her."

"She's moved back to Pakistan. I hear through letters from her now as well as getting the odd phone call."

"Is she really worth it mate? Come on you must have bedded her you're really close."

"We're just best friends. I was in love with her once. I thought she could have anyone she wanted."

I cried in my bed as I'd been listening in. I couldn't believe I'd asked a stranger to marry me and he said yes. I needed an escape from it all so I sneaked out from the hotel texting Jamie saying I'd gone. I had to catch a taxi to the airport and jumped on the next available flight back to Pakistan. I had a favourite lecturer at university of whom I was growing fond of. I missed Ruth and Rachel and kept in touch with them back in America through Skype.

Rachel had taken relationships light heartedly growing up in Arabia and was married now while working in her father's bank. My immediate family were still in Arabia with my brother happily married and a prince with two small children. My phone went, "Hi, it's Jamie. I've got to talk to you. Why did you run out on me?"

"I overheard your conversation with Mark last night over the phone. I really embarrassed myself. I thought he was genuinely nice. I gotta go on my plane now back to Pakistan with my relatives. I'm so glad you've got Cherie but I thought we'd have had laughs on our own again just like the good old days."

"I thought that too. I need your devotion. You're my best, best friend. You've always been in my heart."

"I'll come back for the wedding in September. Cherie seemed really nice. I feel a bit depressed. I've got to go. My family will cheer me up when I get there. I'll call you in two days' time. Thanks for inviting me over."

I soon got back to Pakistan and threw myself back into my university course, biology and chemistry. My lecturer was called Abhu about five years my senior. He was very good looking and would take a lot of interest in me. Every day I walked home to my aunt's and always passed by a desolate looking area and thought back to the days of being enthralled by the Swing Set Park, the massive one in Arabia. The lecturer Abhu would tell me he was into politics. He invited me to a political debate the following week. I actually had an agenda very close to my heart. I couldn't believe that I'd been born into a very desolate run down area. Halfway through the meeting I got a chance to have a ten minute say. I stood up and pledged some money towards creating a Swing Set Park in that desolate area by the ultra-modernised university. They all clapped me as I sat down.

"We would like that too," a lady said, "I have five children and they have nowhere to play."

"Don't you need planning permission?" A dad said of whom I'd spoken to before.

"I'll deal with the right man after the meeting." I looked across at Abhu, he seemed well impressed with me. Abhu came to me afterwards and introduced me to loads of people. We put the wheels into motion to get one built.

"Don't we have a government grant scheme to achieve a local programme sir?" Abhu said to the local mayor.

"Of course we have but the money is very stretched. We'll be pleased for the donation."

"Who do I write the cheque to?"

"The local authority."

"Do you want to publicise the Kumars farm food firm?"

"Not really. I'd rather we were anonymous."

"Fine, but it could be free publicity."

"Put it on the construction notices as it's being built then and put it on a plaque on the gate."

I felt pleased with myself. The months flew by at uni and visiting relations and seeing a Swing Set Park being built gave me a thrill inside. I remember trying to get hold of Jesus while I was there and writing him a very special letter. I wanted to tell him how I felt that I loved him and told him that I always will. I wrote about my new friends at university, my course, my family, and crowed about the new Swing Set Series Park and could he come and officially open the park with his family.

It wasn't until the following year I heard back. His letter made me feel jubilant:

Dear Sherie,

I'm sorry I haven't wrote back sooner. I'm very busy with university and official visits. I miss you and would like to pick up from where we left off. I haven't had a girlfriend since you. I'll make sure I'll come over and visit. You didn't need a ruse to get me to come and visit you. I know you Sherie. There has always been a reason behind why you do everything.

I really love you. I'm glad you got in touch. I'll get hold of you at the university. Have you still got my phone number as I haven't moved. I'm training to be a vet in Arabia.

I know you love being close to your family.

Jesus H William

I could have kissed him. What a lovely letter. I wondered so many times about him and would have loved to know if he still wanted to work in America by the Amethyst room. I had a lot of memories to tell him about and I'd wanted to tell him about my new friends of whom would want to live in America too.

On March 15th 2335 I walked into Williams' university for my class and a big black limousine drove slowly by me and someone shouted out, "Hello Sherie-Marie Kumar!" I looked around and it was Mr and Mrs William.

"Hello sir," and they pulled up beside me standing by the building site.

"Is this your project?"

"Well yes it is. How is Jesus?"

"He's done really well. He'll be over during his Easter break away from his studies."

I pointed to the Swing Set Park being built and said, "It should be finished in a couple of weeks. Is Jesus opening this?"

"Well yes. We've come to see this project and we have a surprise for you in the car." They rolled down the windows and it was my mum and dad. Dad wanted to especially see what the family fortune was being spent on. He actually got out the car with them. I had a little tear in my eye as I gave them a hug. They cried too. "It's so good to see you."

"I've got to go through to class."

"Walk with us and show us your classroom."

"I will dad," and I introduced them to my lecturer Abhu. They all said, "Hello," and shook hands.

"We're sticking around," said dad, "For the next four weeks."

"That's wonderful. Where are you staying?"

"With your mum's sister, Aunty Nola."

"I see her every day now. It's been really good for me to reconnect with old family and old friends again."

"You look amazing," mum said, "In your white jacket. Very professional."

"Well that's how I want to be mum, very professional." I had to give them a kiss, "I'm sorry but I have to go back to class. I'll talk to you later."

They said, "Fine. We're here on holiday and your dad wants to see the Swing Set Park. He wants to see where the family's money is going."

"It'll be brilliant. It'll have two swing sets, a large slide, a roundabout, see-saw and a climbing frame."

"That's brilliant," said dad, "I can't wait to see it."

"If you all excuse me I have a class with professor Abhu and he likes punctuality," and I blushed.

"I think she likes that one." I heard dad whisper to mum.

"We could never keep up with her. I wish she'd find someone to settle down with." Dad said as a parting shot, but I did like Abhu and we were going to the theatre together that night to see Swan Lake. I could have kissed him when he suggested it and that night I put on a sparkling royal blue dress down to my knees. He got us the last box seat and that evening was amazing as he bought expensive champagne just for both of us, on ice, while watching the ballet. I cried at the ending when the swan turned back into being a man after being shot at, and I leaned into Abhu who put his arm around me. This felt really nice and as he took me home in the car we had a discussion about ballets and one I'd like to see next.

"Actually," I'd said, "I'd love to see a musical called Wicked."

He said, "It's better if you've seen the Wizard of Oz and the Return to Oz first."

"I already have at the movies with an ex-boyfriend called Peter."

I needed to write this down in a letter to make Jesus jealous. Then I sent it through the post. No-one knew what I was doing.

A few days later Jesus turned up at the university looking every inch the gorgeous man I ever thought that he was. He was cool and ever so polite with me. My hands were itching to slap him round the face for not hearing the 'I love you' words. "So have you heard about Rachel?" I asked.

"Yes," he said, "We do our banking with Rachel's bank. It was an amazing wedding. Too totally over the top for me and she looked glowing like Cinderella. They had a huge marque for the reception and evening do. I had a whale of a time." I felt instantly jealous.

"It was brilliant when Ruth came out of her shell at the wedding and found a partner. They're still together."

"I actually know that one!" I snapped, "And I knew everything about the wedding as the photos were on the internet while I Skyped my best friend Rachel."

There I thought I've resisted the urge to slap him. "Got anyone you're dating lately Jesus?" He looked a bit vague and shifty at that point and said "I had an affair with a married woman who left me heartbroken."

"Well, were you ever in love with me?"

"Sort of my parents called it puppy love and thought we were cute together but poles apart for I am a Jewish prince and you're a Muslim proper princess."

"I really fell for you but you ignored me when you weren't hounding me for dates."

"That wasn't me. My parents encouraged us to get together that's to help the school's agenda work. You were perfect as the face for the school, It was dad's idea to have you at that press conference. He could have kissed you afterwards," he also wanted to make a dig. I could see it in his face. "So could have I but I think I'd got the cold hard slap after you did it to the photographer. I beat him up as I felt a strong surge of jealousy. Then I got drunk all night."

"I wanted to get pissed myself that night. I was thinking of Jamie who'd always been my best, best friend and I hurt him before then when he finally realised I really wanted to be yours Jesus."

"Really?" he said in a hard voice. "I've heard about your reputation. Poor Peter is still in bits after you've been playing him about and according to Jamie you were going to marry his friend after the first night you met. You're a disaster Sherie. I came here just to congratulate you on the Swing Park and to open it for you just like you asked and I've gotten Abhu fired," he said.

"You can't do that."

"Oh I can. I showed Graham Oliver and he told his brother who runs the university here. If you think you can get into another man's boxers you're deluded."

"Well what about you. You were the main face of the school too and I am incensed that you and your bloody family used me to help publicise the school. I really believed you liked me on all those dates you set up."

"I didn't. I'd have preferred normal dates with you but apparently you didn't need me for that you had Peter and what the hell happened to Luke?"

"He called me mature for my age. You knew he preferred older women."

"Yeah but then you told everyone that he went out with a married woman."

"I bloody love you and always will!" I shouted and Abhu was there next to me. "I'll always be around," he said calmly, "to help you with your studies. I don't care about this prick," he'd said meaning Jesus. Jesus landed a right fist into his face and a left one into his stomach.

"I hate you." He said. Then from nowhere I came up behind Jesus to pull him off Abhu on the floor. I just felt very strong right then.

"How dare you?" I shouted, "It's all been leading up to this. Do you love me? If you don't stop bothering yourself about my love life. It's none of your fucking business and I have no love life with Abhu. You've got it all wrong. I told you that just to wind you up to find out if you really care."

"We're fighting this," said Abhu, "I want my job back. I've done nothing wrong. I've just made a friend with one of my students. Stop acting so jealous."

"I am not jealous," and he went to go for Abhu again and one of his security guards walked him away shouting his head off. "I am not jealous. You're just mad Sherie. Mad."

"I'll take you home," said Abhu. "I hear your parents have come to visit and so has your brother, his wife and kids and your two sisters."

"I need to get to class tomorrow."

"I know you do."

"Look all I want to do is see Graham Oliver to explain about my letter."

"It's too late," said Mary, "I saw it and I always thought you and my son would wind up together."

"Yeah, so did I," and I burst into tears and collapsed into Abhu's arms. "Take me home." I said and he drove me to my Aunty Nolas. At hers I had to explain myself and blurted out, "I'm sorry I'm in a mess that I can't see my way out of. I'm so in love with Jesus and always have been but I feel that I'm pushing him away." Abhu understood.

"I'll get my job back and clear things up. It's so obvious he loves you. I heard the whole argument and I know Jesus's reputation. he loves them and leaves them. That's what the local rag says."

"Well I know he went with my two best friends Ruth and Rachel. Was there anymore?"

"About three and apparently you bedded him too."

"No I never I'm still chaste and waiting. Always waiting for my one true love and to make love for the first time on my wedding night."

"But you are nineteen and totally beautiful."

My eyes glistened with tears and his thumb traced one tear going down one side of my cheek. He tilted my head up and lunged in for a kiss. It was warm and wet, so I moved my head out of the way.

"Not this." I said. "It won't cheer me up. I'm dogged tired and want to be with my family."

"I understand," said Abhu, "But I'm fighting for my old job back and I need you to tell the truth that all we were was a platonic friendship and that I was helping you."

"I'll help you." I said "And between us we've improved the area with a magnificent Swing Set Park."

"But that was your baby," he said and popped his head round the front door and shouted "Pleased to meet you."

Dad said "Pleased to meet you to."

"I'm Abhu Sherie's lecturer," and he shook dad's hand. They walked outside and chatter together.

"I'm going for a walk." I said and pushed passed them. I refused to cry. I wanted to talk to Ruth and Rachel so I went to the universities library to Skype them. I signed on and got hold of Ruth first. She looked amazing so I asked if she was on a modelling job.

She said, "Yes. I've got some time free to talk though."

"Ruth." I said, "I know it was years ago but did you ever bed Jesus?"

She blushed, "I wanted to as he'll always be shit hot. All I can enlighten you on is that he didn't love me enough to want to. That's what he said to me once. We tried dry humping but it just didn't work."

Then she said, "Don't ask Rachel about this she is with family and her husband would find out but I do know that Jesus screwed around with her."

"Where are you two?"

"We're actually in Arabia for an Arabian nights calendar. I get loads of free time. My husband is here watching, ogling all the models he says then he said but you'll always be my favourite Miss May."

I laughed. Ruth and her husband had a really nice gentle way with each other.

"I hate you." I said lightly. "My lecturer Abhu that I've told you about tried it on with me today. I wanted to wipe my mouth afterward but he's such a nice guy and has gotten fired because of me. I have to tell the truth to the college dean."

"Get on it and do it." Ruth said. "Otherwise these things go on and cause fights. I've seen it so many times on set."

"Then that's what I'll do. I'll book an appointment."

"Don't do that," said Ruth, "Just find him in his office and get up the email that caused it all and explain it was a lie to get Jesus jealous. Now that's all you've got to do. Don't try so hard. Sherie you and Jesus are so meant to be."

"I love him. I always have done. Do I have to be honest about Abhu's kiss?"

"He has kissed you?"

"Well yes."

"You shouldn't have owned up to that one."

"I really like him as a friend Ruth. He really takes time out to coach his students." Then I heard a loud cough behind me. "A panel is going to decide his job."

"I'm sorry sir," and I quickly said goodbye to Ruth and turned the computer off. I felt downcast. I really needed to talk with Jesus but he wasn't due back from his other official business in Pakistan he had to do. I really wanted to Skype Rachel and ask if Jesus ever said he loved her. I wanted to be the only one he ever loved.

CHAPTER ELEVEN

That Saturday I was wondering about town with my Aunty looking at the clothes in the shops and at the market stalls outside. I loved the atmosphere of walking down town with loads of people hanging around. You could pretty much tell the holiday makers from those who lived locally. One man had a Hawaiian shirt on and I inwardly laughed and thought of Jamie. "Aunty do you remember me talking about Jamie Lloyd?"

"No. But tell me again."

"He's working to be an ambassador. I'm really proud of him and I'm invited to his wedding in a month's time to a girl named Cherie of whom is really nice. I want a date to go with. I was hoping to ask Jesus as the invite said plus one, but I'm too scared to ask him. I want to ask his mum first if he is free."

"While you're at it she'll tell you if he's been seeing anyone lately."

"I'll do it." I'd said. We continued shopping then I saw an amazing jewellery set of gold dangly earrings, a gold cross on a chain, and a gorgeous gold bracelet and ankle bracelet. A complete set. "I gotta get them and barter for them." I had some notes in my pocket and got him to go down on his price by twenty five percent which was the amount I was willing to pay. "This is going in my hope chest for my wedding day." I said to my Aunty Nola. "I've got a little secret," I'd said. "I've been planning my wedding day since I was eleven years old. I can see myself in a gorgeous orange and red dress with that jewellery set on."

"Let me have a look," and I held up the board with the set draped over. My Aunty looked at it for ages and told me that it looked expensive. "You've got a really good deal on this one," and I put it in my bag with my other purchases. Then someone pushed into me, "Hey watch what you're doing!" I yelled and I made everyone look at me. The man turned round and it was Jesus. He said. "Sorry. I'm trying to keep my head down. I've got the press after me again."

"Well I've got a sound byte just for you."

He said, "Like what?"

"Well you're only here to open another Swing Set. Tell them and more press will show up on the day."

"But this is a tattler."

"Not the man you had a fight with once?"

"Well yes. He got off lightly. I thought he was cracking on to you and I saw red. I love you Sherie," and in the middle of a thriving market he got down on one knee. "Will you marry me?"

"Yes." I'd said and my Aunty didn't know where to look so she just clapped and started crying.

"I've got a ring," he said, "to match that jewellery you've bought," and he slipped it onto my left hand.

"I heard that Jamie's getting married?"

"Well yeah."

"I know Peter has a fiancé now too, someone who was in his class once at school. At least they're all out the way now. I've been waiting for you to ask me out and you never did. You never had to and I loved your company every time I went looking for it."

I said, shaking slightly, feeling a bit faint, "You're amazing."

"Come with me," he'd said "I've booked a table for lunch along here called the Kumars."

"I'm actually getting married," and my legs gave way but Jesus caught me just in time with his big strong arms. "He couldn't have planned this." I said to my Aunty and she said, "I'll leave you in peace and just go to the local burger van," she gave me a lovely smile and walked away.

"In here," Jesus said and he slipped his arm round my waist and a delicious thrill went down my spine.

"You're right. I haven't eaten since breakfast."

"Give your bags to my guard. He'll look after them," so I did and I smiled reminiscing of a time shopping with Ruth and Rachel when I told them to use the bodyguards for the same thing.

We then sat down in a booth and there was music blaring out.

"I had to do this outside," he said. "It's too noisy in here and I've already ordered."

The meal soon came and I spied several samosas.

"You'll make me fat." I laughed and tucked into them.

"I bet you didn't know that I like them too and by the way I want a traditional Jewish wedding."

"But I want...," and he shushed me, "Let's eat and don't worry you can have two weddings with me even three if you want to do it the Christian way."

"You'll get me addicted to weddings," I said happily nibbling away. "This tastes delicious. There's a chili pepper in this."

He said, "I Know. I ordered and I love you very much."

We sat there animatedly talking, mainly about family and I told him what a wonderful place Pakistan was and how I loved my family.

"I'll take you all around the sights tomorrow." I'd said.

"What touristy sights?"

"Some of them, but I want something else to be built and I need to explore wasteland around here but haven't got around to learning to drive yet. Have you?"

"Well yes. What do you want built?"

I said, "A homeless shelter and I can get backing through my lecturer Abhu of whom is passionate about the rights of the local people. I want you involved." And I bowed my head, "Please will you help me, even some of my friends are destitute. There's a political meeting tonight of where Abhu's going and please Jesus help him get his job back. He's a fantastic lecturer. He never touched me. I just wanted to make you jealous."

"He won't get fired. I promise. He might just have to take a long holiday. There's nothing I can really do."

"Do you mean suspension?"

"Well yeah until they get to the truth."

We talked further about our courses and Jesus was fully animated. "I've been on a work placement," he said, "already working in the safari park back home."

"That's brilliant. I've applied all over the world for a placement, even in America. Remember our dream of having a veterinary practice built by the Amethyst Room in America?"

"Well yeah," he said, "Their tenth anniversary is actually coming up and I asked for a tour of the place."

"We were meant to do a tour when we were last there together remember?"

"Well yeah and we had a good speech together."

"I know and I noticed you in Forbes magazine as the wealthiest family in the world ever."

"Well I am a prince," and we shared a laugh. I then had to go back to the university for an evening class and Jesus said he had to go too and on pure instinct, with his eyes gleaming, he put his hand on my waist and gave me a long lingering kiss that was spine tingling. It seemed even better than what I remembered and I kissed him back instinctively running my fingers through his hair. Time just stood still and afterward I couldn't get over the time and raced back on my moped for my class about the dance of the seven veils. I was going to have to nail this for my wedding night in the future. I felt all happy and alive. Jesus and I were going to have to set a date.

The next day I felt so rested that I actually found myself helping out another lady in my class and I told her I was engaged to Jesus. She looked stunned. I said, "Jesus is my fiancé," and I couldn't stop talking about him all day and kept showing off my ring with loads of diamonds on and a massive sapphire. I couldn't stop grinning and that evening Jesus and I were due to cut the ribbon on the new Swing Set Park. I couldn't wait and put on a sky blue and white tied dyed dress with a sash over my shoulder. I then put on grey and blue eye shadow and a nice 'n' soft pink lippy.

At the park there was a handful of photographers and loads of families. I had a knot in my tummy as Jesus and I stood up to face them. I said, "Hello. Welcome everybody."

Then Jesus said, "Ladies and gentlemen here is a new Swing Set Park funded partially by my fiancé and local council."

I said, "This is for the local children of whom have a special place in my heart, as I grew up here."

Then we said together, "We now declare this Swing Set Park officially open."

Then I cut the ribbon and everyone clapped. My mind started racing about my next project to set up a homeless shelter and I blurted out that I had another project on the go to set up a homeless shelter, "As it's been reported that hundreds of people are homeless and living on the streets and rubbish tips in Pakistan."

The families then clapped again and they went through the park's gates. The amenities were soon filled up and I cried tears of happiness.

I walked over to Abhu afterwards and said, "I'm sorry. I know I've cost you your job. If there's anything I can do to help?" and he said, "Stop right there. I wanted to seduce you. That's why I lunged in for a kiss in the end thinking that if I'm getting done for this I might as well do it."

"No hard feelings?"

"You're still my favourite student."

"I'll stick up for you." Said I "and go to that panel meeting before you and explain that I lied and we'll clear this mess up. It's my fault you're leaving."

He actually kept his job in the end and he took me to his next politics meeting. We talked to some wheelers and dealers of whom should be our trustees for the homeless shelter. We needed a lot of money for this shelter to hold up to thirty beds. I'd researched shelters and told them about needing brand new toothpastes, tooth brushes, knickers and boxers for each individual needing shelter. I felt pleased come the end of the night and me and Abhu were officially chair people of my little project.

During my university holidays I went across to the shelter a lot with at least two of my trustees at a time to see how the builders were getting on. The place was to be massive and I realised that lots of other people round town talking to me more. Some people thought that I was really generous and I made the move to the homeless a lot on the rubbish and tried to encourage them to need proper shelter. Some of them were riddled with diseases and the volunteers were endless in coming forward to help these people. My Urdu was getting to sound more like local slang in the end and I learned to have a laugh with those I was trying to help. Some of them were very proud and stubborn people with a lot of mental health problems. What shocked me was mainly homeless mothers with families trying to feed their families, with the amount of help they offered towards getting others decent home cooked food in the shelter.

Decent middle class families we put appeals to for donations regularly coming in with clothes or food. This project I was getting proud of and my work at the university around this time was getting good grades.

In the end I had to find a new chairperson as I neared the end of getting my qualifications for being a vet. By this time the only place that offered me a placement for voluntary work was in America right next door to the Amethyst Room and the original Swing Set Park Jesus and I opened. I'd put in my original letter to the place was to have a month's voluntary work as it was so far away from home. Lo and behold Jesus got the same placement. I was amazed at how much time I'd spent with Jesus and our relationship went from strength to strength. We both agreed that we'd marry as soon as we both qualified as vets. I was dead curious about this Amethyst room and asked Jesus how he managed to get a tour round the place.

He said they asked him and that he learned about holistic healing for a wholeness of health being their top priority, mentally, physically, and spiritually. He actually gave me a brochure about the place and it was massive with every conceivable type of doctor you could think of and at by now twenty years old it still looked brand new.

It was wonderful walking into the veterinary practice that first morning with Jesus on his first day to. We worked side by side as I dealt with the medicines more and Jesus was allowed to do operations. It had all been a team effort in the brand new vets. Jesus told me of the day when it officially opened and reminded me that we both agreed to work with each other at these vets once.

I'd said, "Yes. I remember it well."

"You're really beautiful Sherie," he'd said one evening on a date. "Why don't you try seduction techniques anymore?"

"I want to wait until we're married. I need to know we'd make fantastic lovers. Your kisses send me to heaven and back."

"It's frustrating Sherie. I'd never cheat and I know I'm Jesus the great love of your life with whom everything has to be perfect for. It's a tall order for me to keep up with."

So I surprised him, "Then let's make a date. I want to marry after the next forty days of fasting on the Christian calendar ready for a great feast. I have this idea to blend Jewish, Christian and Muslim marriage ways just for us."

He'd said. "How's that?"

"I wanted traditional Muslim dress code, standard Christian vows, only kosher food and a blend of pop music that I've tracked down to a band back home in Pakistan. It blends a lot of different themes for weddings and ours is the year of a dragon on the Chines calendar. I want one for others to dress up in along our street parade before going to a Mosque for our marriage. I want a lot of fun for us for the whole world to remember as I realised press would be there."

"Wow," he said, "That's a lot to organise."

"That's why I've waited for the perfect wedding planners I'm hiring to take control of."

"I got to ask. Why after fasting?"

"I want to know what unlevened bread tastes like." And I smiled.

"It tastes salty," he said, "Just right for your taste buds. I know what you're like Sherie. You always have to be in control. I'm glad you've included Jewish ways and you didn't get your HRH at school but with me it'll come anyway," he looked wicked with a gleam in his eyes. I asked him if we could pray on this the English way and we said the Lord's Prayer together.

"Don't worry," I'd said to Jesus, "I am never getting everybody to pray to Mecca again," and we laughed clinking our wine glasses together. "To us," we said, "Prince and princess of the Jews."

"I want to contribute to this wedding."

"How?" I asked.

"By whisking you away to the nearest airport for Paris in a chauffeur driven limousine."

"Now that," I said, "You can do and we'll have the Penthouse suite."

"Of course," he said "and finally get to own your ass."

"Ooh," I said blushing madly, "Promises, promises." It was something I'd heard Rachel tease poor Peter with over the years.

"Didn't you say he married one of the girls from school once?"

"Yeah, but I can't recall the name. I think it was Karen."

Our first day was over and I'd seen a couple of dogs and a mad woman talking about her gerbil saying she spoke to him all the time but that he was getting unresponsive as the teeth were not chattering away so much. I had to burst out laughing after she left but I did manage to help the poor pet of whom I'd held in my hands. Jesus had performed a major operation on someone's pet poodle's leg and knitted it back together after being run over. I loved my job. It was brilliant. It turned out to be better than I had imagined. I looked at my left hand several times that day not getting over the fact that I was engaged. One lady that day asked about my fiancé and I pointed him out to her and said he's a wonderful man.

Each day was wonderful and I fell in love with everyone's pets and administered medicines. Then after a week in the gerbil lady came back in and said, "Thank you. My pet's the same as before now."

I said, "No problem. I'm always here if you need help."

Now she got talking about her family. Her name was Wendy and I'd really felt that I got to know her. "I really want to work here long term. I'm looking for a house here in Arizona near to where I work."

"I know of a place set in the suburbs here. It's a large home. I take it you want a family?"

"Well yes eventually at about twenty five?"

"I'd have put you at twenty six."

"I'm twenty one and can't wait to get married during Easter next year."

"Sounds wonderful."

"Look you're the last client for today and I shan't bill you for it," and I laughed as she only came to say thank you. "Can you show me around your suburbs 'cause I take that's where you live?"

"I'd love to show you," and she grabbed her jacket and Wendy led the way.

"I'll take you in my car," I'd said.

"It's really not that far away." Wendy said. "We could walk there."

"I think I know where we're going. Jesus," I yelled, "I'm going. I'm finding a place where we can live together."

"Take me with you. I just got to say goodbye to someone."

He soon came out in his leather jacket and I put my windproof jacket on. We all jumped in my hire car and I drove us to the house. Turned out it was the one I'd been drooling over, with the nice French windows round the back, and a huge bay window out the front. I wished that I could walk in there and peered through the windows. The place was devoid of furniture and the living room, I spied, looked huge. I looked at the sign it said Hooper and Banner, for sale and there was a number underneath. I phoned it straight away as it was only five o'clock and someone answered. "I'd like to make a bid for 52 Woodview Close. When can I make an appointment to look inside the house?"

"In two days' time. What's the best time for you?"

"About half past five." Then we all went for food at a local Thai restaurant and we learned all about Wendy and she said that her house was number 50. "You'll be our next door neighbour."

"I hope so," she said. "This place is full of working middle class decent people and I can tell that you're decent."

I gave a little chuckle, "I'm glad to know that too."

I looked at Jesus "I should have asked how much the place was."

"But we can pay it no matter what."

"Do you mind going halves?"

He said, "Fine."

"We're always equal." I said, "Now this food tastes lovely." I'd wanted to try a different dish I'd never eaten before. Then I soon had to go back to my digs of where Jesus was staying with me. We slept in different beds and I had satin pyjamas. Jesus wore nothing and I ogled his body.

"I really want to get carried away with you," he said.

"Please try massive restraint until we're married."

"But we're engaged."

"My first time has to be special and I need to be in control. I've got something really special planned.

Then Jesus walked to the bathroom and groaned out loud, "I can't put up with this," and I heard grunting and groaning in the bathroom. "Dear Lord this had better be worth it." Then he came back in and went to his bed.

"Next year." I'd said "It's not that long," and I got into my bed strangely feeling lonely. I'd built my first time up in my head to be totally amazing and up there in the moon and the stars.

Jesus said to me, "God I feel lonely. I should have had my own digs."

"I'm sorry but I'm sticking to my plans."

"Then why be quick to put a deposit on that house?"

"I want to live there. It's our plans we made as children."

"I didn't plan on abstinence."

"I did."

"But all you ever did was try to seduce us."

"Yes to get you to fall in love with me."

"I thought that it was for sex. I thought you were gagging for it. That's why you did it."

"I had to find that special kiss that spiralled you to outer space and you did it for me every time."

"As I recall it, it wasn't that often as you dallied round Peter."

"I got confused for a while and then went through a desperate phase to find a fiancé, but really it was always you I wanted. You'd been with Rachel though and then it was Ruth."

"Did she tell you I only did it the once with her and that I lost my virginity to her?"

"I didn't know that. All I found out was that she'd slept with you and Ruth told me she never."

"It was a mistake with Rachel, but I realised after those stupid tests that it wasn't her I really wanted. It was you and only you. Now at least give me a kiss goodnight."

I walked over to his bed and all I could do was be enthralled with his chest and my hands just took control and rubbed over that glorious manly chest. My eyes glazed over.

"This is driving me mad as well you know," and he rammed his tongue down my throat.

"I've got something amazing planned for our wedding night," I tried to tell him this through kissing.

"Enough," he said and I realised my pyjama bottoms were on the floor, "I can't wait any longer," and he picked me up and laid me on the bed. "I'll show you what teasing someone is really about," and he got on top of me. My hands tried to caress his chest again. "You can't get away from just teasing me. I can see that you are ready for this," and he gently caressed my clitoris, "I'll be gentle with you I promise."

My whole body convulsed and then he gently started caressing me with his penis taking his time and his arms pulled me to him tightly. I felt a twinge of pain before a wonderful pleasurable tingling all over me. I was finally so whole and alive with him. This was actually happening and it felt like the earth was moving.

"I'm sorry," he said afterwards, "I should've used protection."

"It's all right my love." I then cuddled into him, but he said to me to clean myself up. I felt insulted.

"Have you got any pads on you?" he said.

"Well yeah, ready for my monthly's."

"Put some in your pants."

"Why?" I'd asked feeling ignorant. I thought that I should've known that one.

"It's got to be your bed now," and I actually had realisation down on my head at what had just happened.

"I don't hate you Jesus. I love you and always will, but I had plans," and then I cried.

"When we marry," he'd said, "We'll have had loads of practice by then and it'll be more amazing." he wiped away my tears as he spooned me and I cried myself to sleep. I didn't know if it was half out of pain, pure happiness or sorrow. in a way it was a mixture of all three.

"It won't be painful from now on," he said and I turned around and said, "Just kiss me till I fall asleep."

CHAPTER TWELVE

The fasting was over and I still liked to pray to Mecca of which I did on the right day. Our wedding was to be on that weekend and I woke up completely happy knowing that I was at my mum's and I hadn't jinxed the wedding by having Jesus with his parents last night.

I got in the bath at six o'clock and had a good long soak for an hour. It was a luxury while I'd had breakfast in the bath luxuriating lovely. I soon got out to a big towel that I wrapped around me. It was my wedding day and I was so excited. I had a phone call from my wedding planner saying that everything was in place. I shivered with excitement as I got dressed. There was to be a street party that I thought of as I slipped into my red and orange dress with a matching sash. I put my make up on and found out my new jewellery. I painted all my nails pedicurely and manicurely. The red looked fantastic. Then I put on flip flops as the sky was warming up outside. My whole family were flapping. My sisters got into their aquamarine tied-dyed dresses as my bridesmaids. Ruth and Rachel came over and they looked fantastic. We had a toast with a non-alcoholic punch. I wanted no-one drunk until the evening.

It was ten o'clock and I looked out the window and laughed really loudly at my dragon that the men were going to carry. They put on my latest favourite tune. They called for me and we all went outside and started dancing to the beat. We didn't have far to walk and I danced by the photographer and cinematographer. I was swaying and turning round to the music while running my sash round my fingers and running with it in the air like a flag. My sisters and my friends knew the dance routine that we did in sync.

We soon got to the Mosque and I spied Jesus's limousine parked nearby ready to take us to the airport.

Everyone took off their shoes and gave them to two workers I hired to look after them on shoe racks with their raffle numbers to match upon picking up afterwards. All the guests magically just parted in the Mosque to create an aisle to walk down and the music made me float down to the front of the place of worship. Jesus looked in total control and his huge grin with an amazing black and white tuxedo. He looked gorgeous as my dad handed me over to him.

The music started playing and everybody sang my favourite hymn, 'Colours of Day'. They sang it very loudly and I couldn't stop grinning. This felt wonderful. Then the music stopped and I started to say my vows of which I repeated with the vicar.

"I Sherie-Marie Kumar, take you Jesus Louis Hartman for my lawful husband, to have and to hold from this day forward, for better, for worse, for richer, for poorer, in sickness and in health, until death do us part." Then Jesus said the same. The vicar soon said, "You may now kiss the bride."

We were kissing for ages and everybody either 'Aahed', or giggled. We broke apart and everyone stood up as we walked by them back outside. The men were quick getting under the dragon again and we all danced to my favourite Kurdish band with my favourite singer Aynur. She stayed with us all evening and well into the morning. It was wonderful and then Jesus and I jumped into the limousine to take us to our hotel.

Later on the next day close family came round to watch us open all our presents that had been put all over the stage in the hotel dance hall. It was exhausting opening presents, but they were wonderful and I wrote a list of whom to send thank-you cards to. I kept the piece of paper in the hotel room. We had wonderful food that had been kosher all weekend. Being a vegetarian I noticed the food going down well and I especially had a well-stocked samosa plated area. I ate enough that weekend and in the evening I got into a dress made up of seven veils and went up to our room with Jesus. My ballet lessons were about to pay off. Jesus eyes looked appreciative as I started to dance to Richard Strauss music as part of the Salome musical. Twirling and saying I kept noticing Jesus's cheesy grin and his head swayed slightly to the music. Back and forth I pranced about the room taking off each veil seductively until I got to the seventh which was my top which I whipped off to unveil my breasts. Jesus came up to me and we danced together even though the music had stopped and he picked me up and laid me on the bed. We made sweet, sweet love all evening. I was in complete ecstasy.

The next day the limousine turned up outside the hotel and drove us to the airport. We were soon on a private jet plane taking off for Paris. I was so excited and elated. Our first stop was the hotel.

"There's an itinerary planned," said Jesus and we went into town strolling leisurely around the shops. The patisserie smelled lovely. It was the early morning bake and my stomach growled.

"Do you want some croissants?" Jesus asked.

"Yes please," and we sat outside the café overlooking a massive park with the Eiffel Tower overlooking us. Jesus saw me looking, "We're going up there this morning."

"This is a very early morning start." I said while yawning. We were in our jeans and jumpers.

"I want to show you the sun rising all over Paris from the Eiffel Tower."

"I'm not used to jeans." I said, but Jesus smiled enigmatically and we were soon walking across the dewy grass. "It's a good job I put socks and sneakers on." I said, but the fresh early morning dew smelled lovely and we went up walking the stairs. Jesus told me that it was better than going up in the lift. We took our time and savoured the view around us as we got higher and higher. I loved the sights and sounds. Jesus pointed out to me where a night club was that he used to go to for dates. "Is it a really good night club?"

"Well yeah. It's called The Moulin Rouge," and he laughed. "The name's a piss take. It's just a regular nightclub with DJs."

I burst out laughing. The uptight part of me thought, "What?" When he said it, until I got the explanation. We were getting higher and higher. I was pleased I listened to the dress code for the day as I was going to put on a nice summer's dress. It took us a long time to get to the top and my head swirled a bit so I grasped hold of the rail. The height reminded me of the trip to Mount Rushmore. I was never afraid of heights but it reminded me that Jesus was. I looked at his tense face. I could tell he still had that fear as he held on tight to the rail too but we still stayed there long enough to see the sunrise all over Paris.

"This is amazing!" I shouted to him as the wind whipped past my ears. He looked at me and he looked really pale. I grabbed a hand and made a move toward the lift. "This'll be better." I said to him and we were soon back on ground level.

"I need a hot drink." Jesus said and we wondered the streets looking at all the shops I wandered where the house was Jamie was living now with his Cherie.

I'd gone to the wedding. It had been very low key and Luke had been there and Jesus too. I got told that Luke Sampson was marrying a Delilah soon, but I never got an invite. The wedding was in a big house and it had been a very chic white lacy dress Cherie wore. Typical, I thought, just like her.

"What are you thinking about?" said Jesus as we sat down to sweet hot tea. I experimented with a strawberry one which tasted very nice.

"I would never get the chance to come back here again after Jamie's wedding."

"I liked that wedding a lot," he'd said, "It had been without too much fuss."

"They had two hundred guests," I'd said.

"It just didn't seem that many," and he looked thoughtful as he sipped his tea.

"You don't expect a specialist tea café in the middle of Paris do you?"

"They're only mimicking the English and trying to do one better."

"I suppose so," I'd said. "Everything is so expensive here. Now all I'm thinking is of the homeless shelter I had built in Pakistan."

"Try not to do that. It's our honeymoon. Cheer up."

"Oh I know. I keep wanting to pinch myself," we walked around again seeing the Arch de Triumph.

The world was waking up all around us and the place was so busy with mainly tourists. Then we went for lunch holding hands to an amazing little café specialising in international foods and lo and behold my samosas were on the menu. I tucked on in. "This is amazing and totally delicious."

Jesus went for a cheese and pickle baguette. "It was a lovely snack." I said to Jesus an hour later when we eventually got up from our chairs.

"I'd love to see the Louvre."

"That's where we're going next and we're meeting up with Jamie and Cherie. Then we are all going to the theatre."

"Won't I get the chance to dress up?" I moaned. He ignored me and said, "It's down here and to the left." We walked through the doors and we took our time and studied each painting one by one. I had to read the brief histories about the art work and their painters. Jesus did the same as we discussed each one. One very mysterious painting was on the wall in a compartment on its own.

"It's a mixture of Cuban modern art and cubanism." I laughed. I said to Jesus, "I'd love to go to Cuba," a bit absentmindedly and under my breath.

"We'll get there," he said.

"At least we've finished university now, and we've got a house to go back to in Arizona. I can't wait." And I flung my arms around narrowly missing an armless statue that was completely white and naked. The icing on the cake was the Mona Lisa and I analysed her expression. "There's a woman always in control hiding many secrets," and I stood there for ages staring at it. Jesus came up behind me for a cuddle.

"Let's get going. I've made dinner plans."

"I can't believe we're going to the theatre. What are we watching?" I had to get over the fact I wouldn't have time to go back to the hotel for a wash and change into a dress.

"It's ok," he said, "We'll just look like tourists," and a shiver went down my spine as he nibbled my ear. I wanted to jump to going back to the hotel and getting into bed.

"Laters," he said then, "Come on," and he held my hand down the steps. Dinner was delicious we had oysters with a light salad. "This is really, really nice," said I.

"I want that dance of the seven veils again every night while we're in Paris darling. I'll feel like I'm being spoiled."

"I might be too tired for that tonight," and I blushed.

"You're better than any other ballerina in the theatre, but this is something you've always wanted to watch."

"Swan Lake." I'd said.

"Rumbled," and he laughed. We soon got caught up with Jamie and Cherie in the lobby. She made me feel out of place in a gorgeous long, strapless, skin coloured dress, with white lines running through it with what looked like baby pearls on the lines. Jesus said to her, "Wow, you must go to the same place Sherie goes. I was going to buy that for her you've ruined her surprise," and he laughed.

"Seriously though," I'd said, "Your dress looks amazing where did you get it?"

"It's not a case of where but whom I got it from," and she laughed, "I trawled the internet for a one off and went to my local boutique, showed them the picture and my designer changed the pure silver baubles for pearls just like I asked."

"I like this. Four friends together," and we clinked glasses with wine from the bar before we went in. Now Jamie had tried to teach me over the years to just sip instead of knocking them back and I took too long over my drink, as Cherie said, "Let's go to our box."

We had the best seats in the house and I picked up the tiny red binoculars and I laughed. "This is to see who's bigger than Jesus." I made Cherie blush but my cheeks were glowing. Then the curtain went up and I became totally mesmerised by the music and dancers. They looked fantastic and I learned a couple of new ballerina techniques while watching it. I watched all the way through with a lump in my throat as I'd grabbed the rail in front of me. I had to put a hand over my mouth at the ending as I sobbed into my hanky. Jesus, I realised, had his arm around me all the way through and I saw a silent tear run down his cheek. it had been a wonderful ballet.

Then when we left we said goodnight to Jamie and Cherie and walked along the Chandra delisay in the moonlight. The little tinkly lights were on running alongside of it. We soon started kissing in front of the moonlight and I shivered with trepidation. Every time with Jesus was going to feel like my first time and it did back in our room.

Jesus and I woke up late for breakfast so Jesus ordered some crepe suzettes for elevenses and I felt like drinking a lot of ice cold water. The suzettes were lovely and I managed two, one with chocolate and one with golden syrup.

"We'll go for a late lunch." Jesus said.

"Perhaps bread and cheese." I said. "So what's on our agenda today?"

"Just wandering around Paris immersing ourselves into the culture."

I had to have a shower before putting on a dress. I'd felt my breasts thinking they felt tender. I was soon ready and we held hands just soaking up the beauty of the place and there were brightly coloured flowers in baskets all over the place emitting wonderful smells as I stopped every now and again to admire them. Jesus told me to look up and he told me that the place we were going in next was called the Montmartre. All I could do was marvel at the architecture and beautiful mosaics. I took a few photos.

"I want some memories, not that I'd ever forget, but we're just a normal couple collecting wonderful times together in photo albums."

We were there for about an hour before coming out into the sunshine.

We went for a long old walk down many side streets before we came along a massive turreted building called the Sacre-Coeur. It took us hours to walk around. It was just as well I had very comfy sandals on with lots of straps on and a kitten heel it matched perfectly with my beige skin tight dress. I caught Jesus admiring me in it several times. That building we went into was huge and I got a crook in my neck as I gazed up to a lot of different styles of architecture and amazing paintings.

It had been nearly three o'clock when we came out. Then we found a rotisserie and Jesus ordered the chicken on it to be put into a baguette, my filling was cheese and pickle. I asked for a small one and before we sat down to eat we walked back to where the Eiffel Tower was to laze out in the grass.

I told Jesus, "I think I've hurt my neck," and he told me to cross my legs as he wrapped his around me to give me a brilliant massage.

"How do you feel about just staying here for an hour?"

"Bliss." I'd said, "My feet are aching," and I led out on the grass and Jesus massaged my feet with an expensive oil that had a dolphin on it. My senses came alive and I tingled all over as he massaged my feet. "Aah," I'd said. "That feels wonderful."

"How do you feel about going in a boat down the Seine tomorrow?"

"That sounds wonderful."

"We'll do a whole day trip," we just lounged around for the rest of the afternoon and we went for ice-creams. There was a certain magic behind the place and I'd been feeling very hot. I asked to go back to the hotel for a shower before tea, "I, Sherie am now a wonderful sex goddess," I said to myself as Jesus had his wicked way with me on the shower and he was a gentleman about it beforehand as he'd asked me, "Voulez-vous couche avec moi c'est soir?"

I'd asked, "How about now?"

"It is this evening." he said missing the point and he jumped on in.

Jesus and I went out for tea and we walked down the Centre Georges Pompidow. I sat down inside an English café that looked very quaint.

"I'd love an English tea." I said to Jesus. "The scones in the window look really fresh and tempting."

It had only been five o'clock so Jesus and I sat down to tea and scones with cream and jam. "Oh that was totally scrumptious. I love English tea."

"You won't want dinner," he said.

"But we would," we said mirroring each other's movements and I dotted some cream on his nose, "I'd better lick that off," I half said to myself and licked it off. "Let's give the English something to gawk at," and we tongued it across the table.

"Let's go back to the hotel room and work this off," said Jesus "And I'll give you a striptease," he cheesily came out with.

Voulez-vous couche avec moi c'est soir?"

"How about now?" and as a pre-appetiser he sang his favourite macho song called 'I believe in Miracles' and I half laughed. The real thing turned out to be better than all the fantasies I'd ever had about him, as I spiralled out of control on the bed after dragging him to it. I didn't have to drag him too hard.

The next day we had an itinerary planned to go to the Sane-Chapelle that was a beautiful church full of stained glass windows. Then we went shopping either hand in hand, or cuddling and kissing that afternoon.

"I really love this. Our honeymoon is totally enthralling and completely amazing."

"I know my sweet. The security guards had to come with us this time as it's a high risk situation going round shops."

"I assumed that we had plain clothed protection. Not one person has asked you for an autograph or a photo Jesus. This type of set up puts me at ease. When I went shopping with Ruth and Rachel once I got really uptight and told them to place their purchases with the bodyguards. That was when we had those three tests."

"You did very well," and Jesus kept his arm around me and nibbling my ear down the Le Marias. He kept me giggling and at every clothing boutique I tried something on but hardly bought anything. I only had plastic on me and in the jewellers we came across I found a really lovely brooch that was pure gold.

"I love that." I'd said.

"It's nearly a thousand pounds. We'll call it a wedding present."

"Would you? It looks awfully like one my grandma used to have. I could wear it sometimes and I'll always think of her." I had tears in my eyes as Jesus put it on my dress between my breasts.

"It looks amazing and totally at one with my dress. You'd think I'd gotten it with it."

"You look totally gorgeous. Guess what's planned for tomorrow?"

"Mmmm," I'd said, "I haven't seen a beach yet. Are we going out of town?"

"Just a little bit."

The next day our limo for the two weeks turned up to the hotel.

"To the river banks of the Sienne please." As we got there I said, "This is hardly a beach."

Jesus laughed and said "We're going on a cruise ship down the river and stopping off at the nearest beach."

"I have my beach stuff handy."

"So have I." said Jesus.

"I love you. I can't believe I'm doing this," and I let the men help me onto the little cruiser. It wasn't as big as I thought it would be.

"We're on our own aren't we?"

"Well yeah."

Once at the beach I caught my breath after having looked either side of me going down the Sienne watching a lot of touristy sites go by me, most of them we'd already been to.

We had a glorious time on the beach in and out the sea glorifying the sun on the beds and I picked up a dark tan on my already brown skin. I'd worn a bright red bikini and could predict for Jesus appreciative glances all day, and what we'd do that evening and he didn't let me down.

"You're amazing." I said as I lay on my back in the hotel room after several poundings to the bed.

The next day we potted about until the evening of when we went to the Palais Garnier, an opera house, advertising Madame Butterfly.

The opera had been amazing. I had a little tear in my eye all the way through.

For two glorious weeks the time flew by. We'd had places to visit every day and we were soon on the private jet taking us back to Arizona. Then from the private hangar a limousine turned up to take us out to the suburbs and I saw the house we bought together. My heart soared into the heavens. Jesus was soon carrying me across the threshold.

The honeymoon wasn't due to be over for another week, but during that week we got a phone call from the vets saying there were permanent jobs there for us. We both said, "Thank you."

At the house Jesus and I christened every room. I couldn't get over how fit Jesus was. Then a surprising phone call came, it was from the President of the United States. We had to check the message several times, but the message was that we had an appointment to visit the President and his wife amongst others from the senate. I wondered if it had anything to do with Jamie of whom had called me about getting his ambassadorship. I laughed thinking it'll be a hoot, but Jesus gave me a grave look.

"Look." I said, "It's lunch with the President of the United States at his home residence. Why look so grave?" But he still looked worried, "Look the security will get beefed up for us. Don't worry we'll be safe." But he surprised me and said "There might be a catastrophe coming."

I said, "Like what?"

"Well it's a first for a Muslim to be there as an ambassador for France."

"So what," I'd said, "It's Jamie, it's all about him isn't it? Being over there being an ambassador for peace. At least he's intelligent enough to speak for himself he doesn't need a translator. He speaks fluent Urdu, French and English. I can't wait to go. When's it going to be?"

"Well that's just it. The message doesn't say when. That's why I feel weird about this," and we checked the message several more times and Jesus began to get on my nerves.

He said to me, "Just get ready." This was the day before we were due to start work full-time. I loved the work next day and realised the receptionist. We had a lovely chat all day until she went home first. Her name was Shelley and I'd told her about the President and Jesus's concerns. She told me not to worry. Shelley seemed very nice and on the Tuesday we had some mail. I snatched up an invitation written in gold pen. "This lunch date is in two weeks' time." I said to Jesus, my wonderful husband. I had to keep pinching myself as the invitation was for Prince Jesus of Arabia and his wife Princess Sherie of Arabia too.

The week flew by and we were soon being greeted at the White house. "I thought we were going to their private residence?"

"We've got to do a tour first and I can trust you to watch your tongue."

Then I realised the world's press was there saying I'd saved many lives out in Pakistan. I thought why do this in America. My brain was getting like Swiss cheese and I couldn't predict what was going on. This put me on edge. Of course the press was there. It had been American press photographing us shaking with President George Rosenheiwer and his wife Sheila Grace Rosenheiwer his first lady they were both Jewish.

I said, "How do you do?"

"Pleased to meet you," they both said. "We've got something we wish to discuss with you."

"Is it about getting more proper Swing Sets all over the world?"

"Well yes. In a nutshell we want loads built in deprived areas all over America. You've shaped our minds about this and would like to take this issue on." Jesus and I sat with them in the main office discussing things. I felt like I was dreaming. It was dream come true and we were due to announce it on television and radio. Jesus looked panicked but I smiled at him and mouthed the words, "I love you, we'll get through this. You can rely on me," and saw him relax a little bit. Then through the doors several ambassadors came in and I noticed Jamie looking as handsome as ever and we both relaxed.

Jamie mouthed, "I've got a script planned," so we let him take over. "I am personally planning a Swing Set area in a deprived part of France." That's what he told the news.

"We're making this a global issue." President George said, "Our next election is all about children and their welfare to prove to the world that our future suffers when not keeping our children happy."

There were loads of lights in our faces and they kept clicking away. The security had to take our party out there pronto for us to get into several limos to go to his house in Wisconsin. This was a totally unreal experience. I couldn't get over it and their house looked totally huge in the middle of sprawling grounds. I couldn't help but think this was amazing and noticed that me, Sherie-Marie William was gripping my husband's hand really tight. We were being accepted into America and they told us that we were to get American citizenship. This was a dream come true and we stood on their lawn for more photographs as we watched the golden helicopter fly away.

I'd said, "Who's that for?" and the President chipped in, "My daughters who now want a Swing Set in our home grounds. Thank you."

THE END

OTHER BOOKS IN THE SWING SET SERIES

Utopia; Shropshire
Come join James and Karen dragging the Saints and Jesus into the 22nd century through love affairs and friendships.

Utopia; Ethiopia
Come join Karen in her quest of Utopia through trials and tribulations in her ultimate goal of having a wonderful marriage to Jesus. Then see how the dynasty of Karen and Jesus survive.

Red socks and pink knickers
THE THIRD TESTAMENT
This is a surprising real life story delving into Karen Genge's life using Bible passages in a brand new way taking the reader to understand an evil way to look at the Bible. It takes you gently on a journey of surprises after surprises in an ordinary girl's life.